The Search for Savin' Sam

WILLIAM CARTER

LONGSTREET
Atlanta, Georgia

Published by
Longstreet Press, Inc.
A subsidiary of Cox Newspapers,
A subsidiary of Cox Enterprises, Inc.
2140 Newmarket Parkway
Suite 122
Marietta, GA 30067

Printed in the United States of America
1st printing, 1998
Library of Congress Catalog Card Number: 97-76266
ISBN: 1-56352-468-6

Electronic film prep by Advertising Technologies Incorporated, Atlanta, GA

Jacket and book design by Jill Dible

For
Tom T.
Who taught me how to tell the tale

And

For
Jana Kay
"Wah-woo . . . Wah-wooo!"

CHAPTER ONE

—

August 1995

THE TOWN DUMP, AN ABANDONED ONE AT THE SOUTH END
of Lula Lane, isn't the best place in the world to bury your
old man.

This is where mine died, though, and this is where he
wanted his body to rot. I couldn't argue; I'm only his son.
The Reverend Sam Lawrence — his newly recruited, spir-
itual-guide-through-life — made the decision for him.

He's dead, too, the Reverend, and in the ground next to
my dad. They hold court, so to speak, over seventeen
other corpses buried all in a row about eight feet down
the slope from them.

I did the digging, and I said the words. I promised I
would and I did. It was a promise reluctantly made after
being held tight in a headlock by Carl the pulpwooder and
being forced to listen to six hours of Reverend Sam's ser-
mons.

I would've kissed ass by then, anybody would've, but I
escaped instead by making a vow to do something I never
really intended to do. But they both knew how it would
end, my old man and Reverend Sam. Those two bastards
knew everything. They probably got drunk and laughed

loud picturing me sweating alone beneath an August sun, dragging dead old people into shallow holes gouged by blistered and bleeding hands.

That was only a few days ago, and only a few weeks after the call from my sister, Amy, that started it all. She told me our old man was sick. He's dying, she said, you have to come home. A message — a command, really — received through six hundred miles of wire.

The next morning I told my boss at the plant I had to leave for awhile and that I would keep him posted (I like that term, keeping someone posted) on what was going on. We'll miss you, Blue, he said, and patted me on the back with his left hand, the one with no thumb or forefinger. He told me a story, with all the gory details, about his mother-in-law's cancer. A horrible thing, he kept saying, as if I were too young to understand and he was in some way preparing me for what I was going to see. He and my co-workers all promised to pray for me and my family. I thanked them and eased toward the door, leaving them all shaking their heads and swapping cancer stories.

"You take all the time you need, Blue," my boss yelled. "Your job'll be here when you get back. You know that."

"Thank you," I called. "I'll keep you posted."

An innocent departure; an implied promise to return after my dad was dead and family matters had been settled. Only a few days, two weeks at most, and I'd be back. The only doubt in my mind at the time was whether my old man really had cancer. How could the meanest son of a bitch in the southeastern United States be taken down by a puny mass of rebellious cells?

Austin Belew . . . excuse me, Senator Austin Belew, my dad, had cancer and I was goddam amazed. What would it be like for him to finally face something of this earth that he couldn't grab hold of and squeeze until it died? I had to see for myself. So I answered the summons.

I decided to make a game of the trip. I pretended I was on my way to Florida for vacation — shades on my face, cranked up stereo, joint in my hand. I was crusin' and started to sing aloud with an old tape of Creedence but quit when I thought maybe the people in the cars behind me could see my lips moving in the side-view mirror. After an hour or so I was stoned and didn't care who saw me singing. I let myself become kind of hypnotized, numb to the blurred landscapes on either side. All I had to do was drive straight for six hundred miles, then take a right.

Five hours later, when the sun began to set, I tuned back in to the world and was once again aware of what a real pain in the ass this trip was turning out to be. I wanted it to be over with. And, for awhile, I actually thought about getting off at the next exit, pointing myself north and traveling right back to where I was before I got that phone call.

Instead, I followed the lure of road signs into the parking lot of one of those combination gas station/restaurant/souvenir and junk places.

There were several cars, three or four campers, and an old Silver Eagle tour bus and a matching van taking up space on the two acres of asphalt. The bus door was open and old people were stumbling out, one by one. The driver stood beside the door and offered each his extended hand, almost pulling the old folks from the bus. Some of them leaned winded against the side of the bus as if disembarking had sucked their strength away.

I sat in my car and watched as canes and aluminum walkers were passed out to their owners. All of the passengers had big, plastic name tags pinned to their chests. The writing wasn't readable from where I was parked, but

I could see bright, red crosses stamped on each tag. When the bus was empty, the driver pointed toward the building and started nodding his head. The old people began to move in that direction, herdlike.

Now, I know that at any given time there are probably a thousand bus loads of senior citizens touring this country. Buses full of widows and widowers going to Las Vegas at a discount. Or couples, gathering together with other couples, getting away from their overgrown children for a while. I've been around groups like those and was always glad for them. They acted like kids.

But this group was different. The ladies weren't patting their hair or carrying big, ugly handbags given to them by grandchildren. No bright, tight polyester pantsuits either. The men weren't wearing fluorescent ball caps printed with sayings like "Old Fart," or "My Wife's a Nun . . . Nun in the Morning or Nun at Night." There was no laughter; no minor arguments. These people were silent except for the sounds of their shoes scuffing the pavement and a collective, ragged attempt at breathing.

I tried not to be noticed when I got out of my car. I kind of eased the door closed and stood still while the eerie group passed. I was impaled by the wandering gaze of one old lady. She was wearing a faded print dress and had bedroom slippers on her feet. Her head was covered by a green scarf. I could tell she was bald beneath it. When she turned her face toward mine, I looked into the eyes of a person who had experienced great physical pain, who was in the middle of it now. I looked into the eyes of a woman who knew she was dying. Her skin was blotched red and her mouth was open. There were Band-Aids in the crooks of both her arms.

This lady studied me, a young man going somewhere,

for a moment. And I wondered if she wondered why I was wearing dark glasses at dusk. Maybe she smiled, I don't really remember. I asked her, "How are you, ma'am?" She just nodded her head, turned, and followed the crowd.

A safety light mounted to an aluminum pole behind me hummed, then stuttered on, coloring everything within reach a pale, cheesy yellow. And for the first time that day I looked to the sky. It was clear to the east — the dark blue of a newborn baby's eye, the color of a southern, summer night. But halfway across, as if divided by a giant ruler, was the edge of a blanket of high, black clouds. Looking west, to the horizon, there was no end to them. Parallel to the storm was I-75 South, my route home. My night would be wet.

As the first winds reached the parking lot, I smelled rain and a hint of lightning. Bits of paper tumbled past me and round, plastic, paper cup tops made bug noises as they skittered across the parking lot. I was inexplicably spooked and hurried into the building.

The fluorescent glare inside was not as comforting as I hoped it would be, and I squinted behind my shades. The store was evenly divided by the round cashier's counter. To the right, from the front door, was the grill and eating area. Along the walls were racks of chips and other fluo-rescent-colored, bagged foods. There were two upright, glass-fronted coolers filled with canned drinks. The cook-ing area was partitioned off by a Formica covered counter. Above the counter hung a four-foot-by-four-foot, hand-painted plywood menu offering hamburgers, hot dogs, and ninety-nine cent breakfasts.

On the left side of the building were rows and rows of free-standing shelves. There were boxes of plastic dinosaurs and stacks of three dollar t-shirts. Novelty license plates seemed to be a popular item and there were too many things to count made from cedar: toothpick holders, toilet seats, bookends, and such. And for some reason, though this place was hundreds of miles in any direction from an ocean, the racks were filled with Florida souvenirs. Anything imaginable was either encrusted with sea shells or printed with palm trees.

A teenaged girl behind the cash register stood staring with her mouth hanging open, toward the rear of the building where the grill was located. A tourist family dressed in t-shirts and baggy Bermuda shorts was standing and staring in the same direction.

Then I heard the voice. And felt it. It boomed and damn near rattled the windows. And I could swear I heard hundreds of matched pairs of ceramic, black mammy salt-and-pepper shakers clinking together on the shelves. Elvis wind chimes, suspended from the ceiling, tinkled in three different tones.

"And finally, Lord Jesus," the voice cried, "we thank You for guiding us safely down this highway as these good people use their last days, their last breaths, to testify as to the glory of Your goodness!"

By this time I'd located the source of the wonderful voice and was staring myself. Back in the grill area, next to the Serve-Your-Self drink dispenser and standing on a plastic, orange chair, was a man with his hands clasped together and his head bowed. His hair was a startling red — it had to be fake, I thought — and he wore a bright-blue, velour running suit. He was no more than four and a half feet tall but appeared to weigh at least as much as I did, about a hundred and sixty pounds. I continued to stare as his entire body inflated and boomed again.

"In Your name we pray, sweet Lord Jesus! Amen!"

He kept his position for the space of three heartbeats and, when there was no response from the other customers, he jerked his head up and glared around the eating area.

"I said amen!"

Another tourist family, cringing in the corners of their booth and looking at the tiny man with a mixture of fear and fascination, offered a timid "Amen." The old, sick people ignored him and milled about looking for direction. Behind me I heard the door open and close as someone sneaked out.

The red-haired man grinned as if he had just created something wonderful. And I admired his teeth. They gleamed white from a face filled with wrinkles and seemed to be as big as thumbnails. He clapped his hands twice, then raised them above his head.

"Awright, awright now! Everbody listen up!" he called from his perch. "We gonna line up real nice and get a cheeseburger! They already been ordered, you ain't gotta worry 'bout that, and all you gotta do is pick 'em up at the end of the line! Carl'll hand out medication when you sit down."

The bus driver, Carl I guessed, was a bald, black man bigger than two normal people. He stood beside the chair holding a tray of tiny paper cups. None of the old people appeared to be interested in food. Most stood, not moving, and others sat heavily in the booths. Some were still panting from the effort of walking from the bus. One old man stood in a corner, staring at his reflection in the plate-glass window, scratching his forearms.

When no one responded to his instructions, the small man clapped his hands once again and bellowed, "Let's eat, people! Come on now, we ain't got much time!" This time I noticed the thick, gold chains he wore on each wrist and the matching one about his neck. He leaped from the chair like a small boy jumping into a puddle of water and began guiding people toward the counter, prodding and chiding.

"Now Miss May," he told one birdlike, old lady, "you know a little grease never hurt nobody! Get a cheeseburger, now!"

He grabbed a tall, skinny black man by the arm and pulled him from a booth.

"Curtis," he said, "I been told you could eat a whole hog by yourself 'fore you got sick! Come on, now, you gotta eat!"

He continued this, with a little help from Carl, until all of the bus passengers were lined up at the serving counter. With a tug on the left sleeve of his blue suit, he exposed a clunky, gold watch and studied it for a moment. I could see his lips moving as he counted.

"We got forty-five minutes, y'all," he instructed. "Enjoy your supper!" He whispered something to Carl, then walked over to the booth containing the worried tourists. They didn't look too happy at his approach.

At that exact moment I was hit with an uncomfortable sense of déjà vu. I knew the short, red-haired man from somewhere. The walk was familiar, the voice was familiar. I'd seen those big, white teeth before. But the time and the place and the situation would not come to me. The harder I tried to remember the man, the less I remembered.

I've never been too excited about "running into" people I'm supposed know. Most of them didn't know me anyway; they knew my father. I decided to take a piss, buy a cold drink, then get back on the road as quickly possible.

The teenaged girl at the register had lost interest in the

scene at the grill and the tourist family was admiring a rack of silver-plated spoons stamped with state names.

"Oh my goodness!" the mother squealed. "They got Utah! Look honey, Utah!" The man grunted and selected a two-pound pecan log from a nearby shelf.

"Can I help you, sir?" the cashier asked me.

I shook my head. "Uh, no. No, thank you. Just lookin'," I told her.

She seemed relieved.

I found the rest room and went in. It was divided into two rooms. The entry area contained a counter with two sinks and there was a wall-mounted, air-blowing hand drier. Above the sinks was a big, square mirror. I went through the other door and stepped into one of the stalls.

While I peed, I read the walls. It was scary. I felt as though I'd stumbled into some weird, netherworldish dimension and was spying on private and personal messages of the insane. I was entertained, though.

I finished, zipped up, and stepped out to wash my hands. After removing my shades, I splashed water on my face, forgetting there were no paper towels. I pulled out my shirt tail which worked just as well. While I stood with my face covered, patting it dry, the door squealed open.

"Hey there, boy! How ya' doin'?" The voice bounced off the tiled walls many times then hung still, expecting a reply. I had no choice.

I uncovered my face and replaced my shades before looking up. Standing in the entrance, holding the door open, was the short, praying man in the blue suit. He grinned at me then stepped into the room. The door swished closed and he held his hand out to me in greeting.

"How ya' doin', boy?" he repeated.

"Alright, I guess. Thank you. How are you, sir?" I took his hand. He was just about a foot and a half shorter than me and I could see the top of his head. His hair was red, alright, and very thin. The exposed skin reflected the fluorescent light and enhanced the peculiar spiral growth pattern of the hair. It looked like an old-time baby doll's head.

Transplants. I was mesmerized.

"Reverend Sam Lawrence," he proclaimed, pumping my hand.

A few seconds passed before the spiraled hair released me and I was able to respond to the man's introduction.

I blinked and said, "Pardon?"

He let go of my hand and took a few steps back. Wary steps.

"I said my name is Sam Lawrence . . . Reverend Sam Lawrence. What's wrong with you, boy? Why you in the bathroom with your head covered up and wearin' sunglasses? You on dope, boy?" He moved a few inches closer to the door.

"Oh no, sir!" I exclaimed. "I've been drivin' a long time. Just a little tired, I guess." There was no way he could discover my lie. The last of the evidence was in ashes beside the road about fifteen miles north.

Reverend Sam must have decided I was okay because he winked at me and grinned.

"Oh well, then," he said. "I understand."

And in that instant, I knew who he was. He was "Savin' Sam, the Trailer Man," a once well-known and very popular celebrity in the entire state of Alabama and the southern half of Georgia. He used to own a chain of mobile home sales lots, and his salesmanship and bad commercials were legendary. I've stayed up late many nights, drinking beer, smoking dope, and flipping channels waiting for one of Sam's sixty-second ads to appear. Wild parties I've been at were silenced by an announcement that Sam was on television.

When I saw him standing there in that rest room, grinning at me, a whole flood of really bad TV ads came back to me. Most were predictable; the ninety-nine-ninety-five, thirty-days-same-as-cash, no-payment-till-Easter kind. But every week or so Sam was inspired. One in particular showed an upper lower-class couple entering a sixty-foot double-wide. The man was red from the sun and wore a monster truck t-shirt and a Copenhagen snuff cap. His wife was tanned, long-legged, and wore short, short cut-off blue jeans and a tube top. She had big tits and blond, almost white, hair. They strolled through the trailer admiring the shag carpet, the ceiling fans, the "thrown-in-for-free" stereo systems. They "oohed" and "aahed" over the master bedroom with the mirrored closet doors and pretended to luxuriate in the dry, whirlpool bathtub. And in the kitchen they stood beside the pine dinette, surrounded by new appliances, and discussed their situation.

"Oh, honey," she said as she grabbed his hand and gazed into his eyes. "This is what we always wanted! This is our dream home!"

He hung his head and shuffled his feet a bit. "I know, baby, but the payments on somethin' this fine would surely be too much for us. We could never afford it."

Then there was a close-up of the lady's slightly pouting, teary-eyed face. She blinked her blue-powdered lids. A switch to the man's face showed him to be embarrassed at not being able to buy his woman what she wanted.

But then, as if sent from Heaven, a booming voice, a sign of hope, filled the kitchen.

"Wait a minute! Don't give up so quick! You done come to the right place, 'cause I understand!"

The couple's eyes rounded in surprise and the camera turned to the twenty-one-cubic-foot refrigerator. The door flew open, banging against the base cabinets, and Savin' Sam stepped out, covered with fake snow.

"Oh my goodness! It's Savin' Sam!" the woman squealed.

"That's right," said Sam, "and I'll go to any extreme to make a deal with you!" He brushed snow from his shoulders and bounced over to the couple, putting his arm around the woman's waist. The top of his head just reached her tits. He looked up at her and grinned.

"Darlin'," he purred, "Ol' Sam can make all your dreams come true!" Then he winked into the camera.

As the scene faded, a voice-over proclaimed: "Savin' Sam . . . He understands."

Not all of Sam's commercials were as wonderfully bad as this but they came close. And for years and years he could be seen and heard everywhere. He became rich and, believe it or not, influential. Everybody courted Sam and during election years a word from him could make or break a candidate. My father, a United States senator, actually sat in on photo opportunities and attended barbecues with the trailer king.

Then Savin' Sam disappeared, faded away, followed by a hint of scandal. Taxes, I recalled, and a few other, more unsavory things.

Sam cleared his throat, pulling me from my memories, and asked again if I was alright.

"Yeah, yeah. Excuse me," I said, "I'm a little surprised. You're Savin' Sam, the trailer man."

He seemed pleased at being recognized, but also a bit

embarrassed. His ears reddened and he studied the floor for a second. Then he looked back up at me and spoke for the first time in a normal tone of voice.

"That's right, that's right. But I don't sell trailers no more. Instead of savin' money for people, I save souls for Jesus. I'm doin' what He told me to do. He's sent me on a mission." He tapped a finger on the plastic name tag pinned to his chest.

There was a glare from the light and I had to tilt my head to read. In one corner of the tag was a red cross, just like the ones I had seen in the parking lot. At the top, in black letters, was his name. Below that, in a red matching the cross, were the words Cancer Casualties for Christ.

"This is what I do now, boy," Sam told me in answer, I guess, to the question on my face. "I go to hospitals and old folks homes, lookin' for people dyin' from cancer. After a little talkin' most of 'em are ready to testify, to witness. Then I take 'em on the road, in that bus outside, to churches and revivals all over the south." He paused, waiting for reply. When none came he began to speak again, but his voice had lost its humbleness.

"They like it!" he shouted. I jumped. "People come from all over to look at 'em and hear 'em tell about how bein' sinful gave 'em cancer . . . made 'em sick! They feel like they're doin' somethin' good before they die; spreadin' the word, testifyin'!" He began to pace. His running shoes squeaked on the tiled floor. I stood and watched, my uneasiness growing as I struggled to recall everything I'd ever heard about Reverend Sam and his mysterious disappearance from the public eye.

"I take care of 'em, too!" he proclaimed. "Nobody else does! Most of them people out there don't have young'uns to look after 'em, nor any kind of family! Some of their families don't even want 'em no more! They was all just layin' in them beds, dyin', 'fore I got to 'em! Most of 'em couldn't wait for me to take over their bidness for 'em!" Sam was sweating, pacing, and I was easing toward the door.

"Lotsa people say I keep them checks for myself! Hell, I feed 'em, give 'em their medicine! We stay in nice, clean motels most of the time! It takes a lot of time, handlin' all them insurance papers when they die!"

He spun around and grabbed my arm.

"There's really not that much money left, after they're buried, you know." He was calm now and he patted my shoulder. "It's all for Jesus, anyway," he said.

I saw a chance to escape. "I'm sure you do real fine work, and it's good to meet you," I lied. "Well, looks like rain, it's dark, and I'm runnin' behind. I gotta go." The door swung open with a push from my shoulder.

Sam had already forgotten me, it seemed, and stood playing with the gold necklace about his neck. One step forward took me to freedom, but before I could get away I heard the preacher call to me.

"Wait! Wait a minute, boy!" One part of my brain said to keep walking but the other part, the one with my Southern manners, made me back up and stick my head around the open door.

"Sir?"

"Your name, boy. What's your name?"

"Blue," I said. "Blue Belew."

Sam cocked his head and rubbed his chin. The gold bracelet twinkled.

"Belew," he muttered, then repeated. "Belew." Then he smiled. I flinched a bit. The connection had been made.

"You any kin to Austin Belew, the senator?"

And though I've been tempted many times to deny the relationship, I never have. Blood, I guess.

"Yeah," I admitted. "He's my father."

"Well, I'll be damned!" said Sam. "I shoulda' known! You look just like him now that I think about it! How's your daddy doin' these days? He handlin' retirement awright?"

"He's . . . he's fine," I said quickly with labored nonchalance. For some reason I feared giving this man any inkling of information about my old man. I didn't think Sam needed to know about the cancer.

"Fine, huh?" he said, rubbing his chin. Then he tilted his head and looked at me for what seemed like hours. I could swear he was digging in my brain. "Your daddy's a good man. I know him well; helped him get elected a few times. Me and him think just alike." He studied me again. "You sure he's okay?"

"Yeah . . . yeah," I stammered. "He's fine. Doing real good."

Sam nodded. "Well, you have a good trip, boy, and tell your daddy ol' Sam said 'hey' and hopes he gets to feeling better." And then he grinned and laughed.

I turned and walked away. Past the shelves loaded with plastic things. Past the girl at the counter riding the clock. And past the old, sick people sitting and staring at uneaten food. That one old man was still looking at his reflection in the window, scratching his arms. I remember wondering what he thought about . . . or if he thought at all.

A full storm waited for me outside. It felt good getting wet as I walked to my car. There was thunder and lightning and the rain stung and was cold, but it made me clean. I took my shades off and slid into the driver's seat, immediately comfortable and in control again behind the wheel of my own little world. Every rip and tear in the upholstery, the smells of mildew and old, spilled beer, the tap-the-gas-twice, pause, tap-again-then-turn-the-screw-driver combination of starting the engine.

The windshield was fogged so I wiped dry a head-sized hole. Nothing was visible beyond the reach of the head-lights, but with every flash of lightning the building, the bus, and the blacktop parking lot jumped out at me in stark, two-dimensional detail. I was safe, though, and anxious for the anonymity of the road.

For some reason, fighting the wheel and the rain relaxed me and made traveling easy for awhile. Not even the trac-tor-trailers speeding past in the blinding rain unnerved me. For a hundred miles or more I drove in an almost dream, cocooned in my car, aware of nothing but happiness at having escaped Reverend Sam and his inquisition.

I spent a few miles worrying about whether or not I'd given anything away. About whether Sam somehow divined my old man's condition by the way I was stand-ing, maybe, or in the number of times I blinked my eyes. He was capable of it. And then I tried to figure out why I was worried about it. I never did come up with any answers, though. A couple of hours later the rain stopped and the moon came out. A full moon that seemed much bigger and closer than it should be. A moon to make you glad you saw it. I pulled over, got out of the car, and stood looking up at the sky.

The moon made me dizzy and I remember wishing I was the only one in the world who could see it at that moment. Kind of a secret between me and the night. The only thing to mar the moment was a green sign, fifty yards in front of me, indicating my exit from the interstate was six miles ahead. I could still feel a faint tug from behind me, pulling me north, and I wondered if it was too late to turn back. An hour and a half south of here was the town where I grew up. There was a moment of apprehension — well, let's call it panic — but not enough to make me abandon the trip. I nodded at the moon, thanking it for the display, then got in the car and drove the six miles to my exit.

Highway 280 west is a state road connecting two major interstates; one in Georgia and the other in Alabama. The three hundred miles between them are ignored by half the travelers — the ones who weren't born along that stretch, the ones just passing through. But the other half — the half that has lived its life there, the half with many generations of deep Southern blood running through its veins — knows those three hundred miles to be something special. Wonderfully special . . . or terribly special.

And I felt it. I felt it when I turned right off I-75 and onto 280 west. A little thrill of electricity; a faint hum of energy born only of longing ran through my body. It was like passing through a thin, invisible wall separating this band of blacktop from the rest of the world. And, I'll admit it, I almost cried. I'd been homesick and didn't even know it. Three years is a long time to deny anything. For awhile I felt good enough to forget my reason for being here.

It was late and I had the road to myself. I rolled my window down and took in great gulps of cool, rain-washed air. The heavy, pregnant smells of fresh-turned, damp red earth and south Georgia pine flooded the car. And then I did cry . . . but only for a minute or two. I couldn't help it. Maybe it's because when I was born those smells, even from within the antiseptic walls of a hospital, were the first to enter my body. They mingled with my blood, I think, and seeped into my cells. Something inside me was triggered by those smells and, whatever it was, made me feel good.

I drove with my hand stuck out the window, cupping the wind. And from deep within the moon-cast shadows of the pine forest I could hear cicadas trilling; a sound I had forgotten. A few miles later the smells changed to those of the swamp. Wet, secret smells that at first can take your breath away; make your nose wrinkle. But after a moment the body accepts these smells; the smells of growth, the smells of birth. Every quarter-mile, it seemed, I glimpsed pairs of silver-green eyes: possum, deer, other creatures, frozen at the edge of the road by my lights. Fine companions for a fine nighttime ride.

And as the road, my road, welcomed me, I realized I was happier than I'd been in three years. Long-forgotten landmarks; some seen only in silhouette, others not seen at all, flashed past — part of my reunion.

And just as I was beginning to wonder if this was going to work, if maybe the trip was worth the time, my happiness vanished to be replaced by a peculiar dread. Ahead of me, about a quarter-mile on the right, was a tiny road sign, glowing green from the lights of my car. I already knew what it said and slowed down, not wanting to read it yet, not wanting to ruin the ride.

When I was fifty feet of so from the marker, I pulled to the side of the road and got out of the car. Looking south, beyond a wide stand of pine, I could see the glow of streetlights obscuring the night. And as I walked toward the sign the moon went away, hidden by a band of black clouds. The rain came just as I began to read.

WELCOME TO DURA, GEORGIA Pop. 2880

I was home.

Chapter Two

—

Dura is a weird town in the light of day. At two in the morning, and a rainy one at that, it's weird and strange.

It lurks.

I remember standing at the city limits sign when I was eight or nine years old wondering about the population figure and who kept up with it. There wasn't a little shack beside the road housing some old man with an adding and subtracting machine. That would've been perfect. Nor was there some electronic device scanning the passing cars and their occupants, keeping count of those trying to flee. And there was nobody with a can of white paint to run out and change the numbers every time a new baby cried or someone drew their last breath. The figure stayed the same. Just like the town.

There's a curve to the right in the road, through two hundred yards of pine forest, that keeps the town hidden until it leaps into view. And . . . bang! You're in the middle of a bunch of buildings. Halfway through the curve, at the edge of the woods and mounted fifteen feet high on three telephone poles, is a huge billboard showing a happy family of four standing in front of a Beaver Cleaver suburban home. Beneath the family is printed a message:

"WELCOME!" it screams. I knew without looking there was another message printed on the back. It says: DON'T BE A STRANGER! Hysterical begging, it seems. This sign, unlike the one filled with facts and figures, is kept new and fresh looking. I used to ask people if they didn't think it was kind of misleading, the happy family sign, but never got a verbal response. Only looks. Weird ones at me and furtive ones around the area to see if anyone had seen us talking together. I was in my late teens before I learned not to question the veneer of health and well-being surrounding our town. Anyway, the sign, lit by four perpetually burning 150-watt bulbs — paid for by the Dura County Chamber of Commerce — greeted me with all of its false advertising.

Then there it was.

Dura.

In the early seventies a movie called "The Exorcist" was released. It was a big hit and everybody saw it. Except me. My mother told me it was not something a child (I was twelve) needed to see. What she didn't know was that I had purchased an already well-worn paperback copy of the novel from a friend about a year before. A book of nightmare. But it was the poster for the film that made a lasting impression on me. The picture showed, in silhouette, a man standing in a pale, misty yellow light with his back to the camera. He's outside at night, on a sidewalk, wearing a fedora and a black topcoat. In his left hand is a valise. He's a priest, I think. What sticks with me is the way he's looking at the building before him. The window on the second floor holds his attention. He'll be in that room soon, he knows, dealing with whatever's up there. And while he might not want to, he's going into the building, climbing the stairs and opening the door to that second-story bedroom. Just because he knows he has to. He pauses for a few moments before entering, I think, to have one last taste, one last feel, of his peaceful, monster-less life.

Or maybe he's just scared.

As melodramatic as it may seem, that's what I thought about, what I felt like, when my wheels rolled me into town.

Main Street is three blocks long. Three blocks of post-card-perfect, brick storefronts and covered sidewalks. A Main Street to define all other Main Streets. The century-and-a-half-old gas street lamps, hung with baskets of fresh-cut, summer flowers and now casting electric light, are the first indications this town is unlike most others.

I remember many summer days and Saturdays, when I was a boy, walking beneath the shade of the covered side-walks on this street. A fistful of change didn't last long because anything I wanted could be found right here in downtown Dura. Malls, shopping centers, and discount stores were places I'd seen advertised only on television. I couldn't imagine anyone wanting to drive the fifty or sixty miles to Columbus or Albany just to buy something. My teens came before I realized the absence of convenience stores and super groceries was not normal.

Main Street widens, then dead-ends on the third block. We've always called it the town square. There's only one way in and one way out, though. I was always reminded of those box canyons that the cowboys in the movies used to trap herds of wild mustangs. There's no escape.

City Hall is on the square, facing in like all the other buildings on this block. Joined to it on one side is the courthouse. On the other side is the Dura County Sheriff's Department. These three buildings squat like a huge brick-and-marble mother hen, protecting beneath her wings all the brick biddies on the block. The biddies that make Dura what she is. There's a bank — one much bigger than a town this size needs — two real estate offices, two insurance companies, Dura's weekly newspaper, a mortgage company, four certified public accountants and an office supply store. And I don't want to forget the lawyers. Eight of 'em. And all kin to me. Three uncles, an aunt, a brother, two first cousins, and a second cousin. My father's office is on the second floor of my uncle's law office. Even retired U.S. senators need their own space.

I have a lot of relatives on Main Street. The mayor, the newspaper editor, two of the CPAs, several insurance agents, and the bank president. As a matter of fact, the Belew family is involved with or owns damn near everything in Dura. And I do mean everything. The Tattooed Rooster Bar and Grill is the only truly independent business in town. Of course, the family doesn't own the government buildings; but having claims on the people inside them counts for something.

In the middle of the square is a small park, and in the middle of the park is a statue. I left my car in front of the courthouse and walked across the street to stand at the base of the monument. The granite spire rises twenty feet and its sides are engraved with Confederate flags entwined with magnolia leaves. Atop the spire is the frozen stone figure of a stern-faced, handsome man, peering north and cradling a rifle in his arms. He's Aubrey "Buck" Belew, a rebel's rebel and my great-great granddaddy. Myth and legend claims he single-handedly drove back Union forces and saved this one bit of Southern soul, Dura, from certain degradation at the hands of Yankee barbarians. William Spires, town founder and the richest man in Southern

Georgia, was overwhelmed enough to offer, as a prize to Buck, the hand of his beautiful daughter, Miss Ambrosia. Thus began the dynasty and a century-long pedigree of brains, beauty, and power much envied and coveted by other, less fortunate, Southern families.

Looking up at Buck I remembered all the times, as a child, I pretended he would leap off the spire and stride through town as my point man. People would cower or scatter before his rock rifle as I directed him to wherever I wanted him to go. I used to think of him as my only friend in this box canyon. That was a secret, and Buck and I kept it between ourselves.

Maybe it was fatigue from the trip or maybe it was a trick of the light shining through the early morning mist, but for just a moment, I thought I saw those old stone eyeballs turning in their sockets to peer down that old stone nose. And then . . . then I saw those stern stone lips curl into a small smile of welcome.

"Hey, Buck," I said.

Another illusion of the light and he was once again looking north, ever vigilant for intruders.

By the time my visit with Buck ended, I was soaked and cold. As I got in my car, I noticed someone looking out a window of the sheriff's office. Taking note of this strange man in a strange car with a strange license plate, no doubt. I waved and the face disappeared.

I knew where I had to go, so I left Main Street and took a right onto Ambrosia Road, toward the hospital.

It took a lot of effort, leaving neutral territory.

After a few blocks, downtown dwindled and became residential. Four-acre front lawns were the norm in this part of Dura, and both sides of the street could've graced the cover of any architectural or gardening magazine. Old

Southern money. I've been in all of these homes at one time or another. For parties, weddings, funerals, or just to hang out. I've sat in high-backed wicker chairs on the white-columned verandas of these houses. And I've roamed the halls of these mansions admiring the dark paneled walls adorned with oil portraits of long-dead Confederate general ancestors. I dated the daughters and drank beer with the sons of the people who own these homes. Of course, that was before I became "a little strange." Now, even though I'm sure I wouldn't be turned away — manners, you see — I don't think I'd really be welcomed anymore. Tolerated, but not fully accepted.

This part of Ambrosia Road is canopied by the arms of ancient oak trees; a living tunnel that ends at the wrought-iron gate to the manicured expanse of my family's home. A quarter-mile before that gate is reached, on the left, is the Anna Belew Memorial Medical Facility, a ten-bedroom private hospital. Anna Belew was my great granny. There are no signs, no indications, of this being a place of healing. Better to keep the masses away, I suppose. No need for guards; those not allowed know who they are.

It's an old antebellum mansion, the hospital, that appears never to have transcended the nineteenth century. To see a white-suited plantation owner directing slaves from the front porch wouldn't have really startled anybody. The surprise comes from discovering the degree of well-funded, state-of-the-art, medical technology hiding behind its walls.

Once a private residence, belonging to my great granddaddy, the mansion was where Anna Belew spent every minute of every day of the last thirty years of her life. She went crazy, the story goes, when her husband died, and she wandered the halls wearing his old, brown overcoat, her iron-gray hair just brushing the floor, muttering to the portraits on the walls and shrieking at the sight of other human beings. A full-time physician was hired, along with a nurse or two, to keep her from harming herself. She died in 1922; still wandering and muttering and shrieking.

The doctor and nurses stayed, with blessings and money from the family, to maintain the mansion as a hospital. Only the chosen, the Belews and their offspring, benefit. And though it's mainly a place of research now — run by the good Dr. Armond Belew — the old and the feeble, the sick or the genetically defective, or the just plain tired members of my family retreat here to heal behind its heavy oak doors. Some never come out. But that's okay; the best in medical aid is here. And it's gossip-free; unlike the halls of the county hospital.

The windows were full of light and the drive was crowded with cars. I decided to park on the street and walk the hundred yards from the gated entry to the front door. Anyway, my faded yellow Pinto would've clashed with the muted grays and the gleaming blacks of the finer automobiles.

As I made my way up the drive, careful of the rain-slicked brick, I glimpsed glowing tips of cigarettes and the shadowed faces behind them in several of the cars: drivers or personal aides or body guards. Some of those faces turned toward me, pausing in mid-drag, to assess the threat. Others were only curious. But nobody stopped me. If I've inherited anything from my family, it's a way of walking and carrying myself as if I belonged exactly where I was. Besides, I'm told I look enough like my father for there to be no mistake as to my bloodline, even in low-level, landscape lighting.

The front steps are brick and sixteen feet wide. I

remember playing on them when I was a kid while waiting for my mother, when she was able, to end her weekly visits with whomever was checked in at the time. It wasn't play exactly — more like banishment.

For some reason my parents decided the age of six was old enough for me to make social calls on barely breathing people who didn't even know I was there. My first such visit was to one of my great uncles. I'd been dressed in a little boy's, navy-blue suit with a red bow tie and was very excited. The nurses all told me how cute I was and a man in a white coat shook my hand. We walked up the carpeted stairs to the third floor, then to the far end of the hall, and my mother knocked on the last door. Nobody answered but we went in anyway. The drapes were open and the room was bright. There were flowers on the large wooden chest of drawers and a stuffed, toy bird dog sat in a rocking chair by the window. The bed was huge, framed by carved, wooden posts and covered with a multicolored quilt. Beneath the quilt was a lump. Kind of small, really, not anywhere near grown-up sized. From where I was standing, just inside the open door, I could see what appeared to be tufts of gray hair, screaming in contrast with the stark white of the pillow case, peeking out from the quilt. No machines, no gleaming metal IV stands. I was a little disappointed.

"Uncle Ames," my mother called out in a voice somewhere in between a whisper and a normal speaking tone. "Uncle Ames, I've a surprise for you today. You have a special visitor."

The lump didn't respond and I thought maybe Uncle Ames was hiding behind the dresser or under the bed. Before I could squat down to look, my mother took my hand and led me to the center of the room.

"Uncle Ames," she half-whispered again.

And somewhere deep within the quilted landscape of the bed, somewhere near the pillow, came the sounds of things I'd imagined lived only in the dark corners of unused closets. Sounds best never heard by six-year-old ears.

"Schoooonck . . . schoooonck . . . schoooonck."

I tried to warn my mother, to scream for her to "Run, Mama, run!" but my lips wouldn't move, my throat was closed.

She was brave, though, or unwilling to show fear in front of her baby. And even though I was paralyzed, as rigid as a rock, she was able to pull me toward the headboard to stand beside the bed.

"Sometimes you have to get his attention," she said as she tugged the covers back from the pillow.

I screamed.

Uncle Ames, a milky-eyed, drooling, drawn-up, toothless, gray-haired old man — the oldest in the world, it seemed — screamed in response.

He screamed for a long time and flailed about the bed with his thin, bony arms flapping above his head. I could see his gums glistening and his tongue rolling about his mouth like a pale, white grub.

A nurse appeared from nowhere to calm him and to order my mother and me out of the room. I was ordered out of the building to await my mother while she took care of damage control.

Never again was I expected to visit. Oh, I made trips, but my job was to sit on the steps and wait. They're big steps but seemed much bigger then.

There's something about the sound of footsteps on a wooden porch floor. It's a portentous sound that can cause otherwise stoic people to leap from their easy chairs and go scurrying to the front window to peep out from behind the safety of the shades. It's a sound to be heard from across the street; carried on the breeze of a warm summer's evening while sitting on your own porch, followed by the squeal of rusty hinges on a wood-framed screen door just before it slams shut. All in all, it's a good sound; a sound of small towns. But not here; not on this porch on this night.

My footsteps seemed barely to have the chance to echo, but fell flat and muted. The white, wicker rocking chairs and the overflowing baskets of ferns sat like props upon the porch and lent no warmth to my arrival. And then the door tried to intimidate me. It's a massive white thing with a polished brass knob and knocker. A handsome door, really, but more like a sentry than a slab of wood. I could've stood there for hours, I believe, matching it glare for glare. But instead I reached out, with only a small amount of fear, and turned the knob before the door had a chance to animate itself and deny my entry.

For a second I was six years old again. The foyer was the same, as were the thick, patterned carpets protecting the walnut floor. The paintings on the wall hadn't changed either; the same dead relatives stared out from the same gilded frames. There was a desk, though, and behind it sat a young lady in a severe blue suit. And she wasn't smiling.

I cleared my throat and said "Hey."

"Is there something I might be able to help you with, sir?" she asked, though I could tell by her tone of voice that she had very serious doubts about it. The "sir" was kind of coughed out as if it were a small bone lodged in her throat.

I couldn't blame her, really. My hair was matted down

by the rain and I wore blue jeans and a gray pocket t-shirt. And the cigarette I was trying to light probably didn't help my appearance much, either.

"Yes ma'am," I said, "I'm here to see the Senator. I'm his son, Blue."

The girl was a professional and didn't react physically to my claim, but there was a slight shift in attitude.

"Oh yes, yes, of course," she replied as if she'd known all along who I was but had momentarily forgotten. "Would you wait for just a second, please?" She picked up the phone and punched a button, watching me but pretending not to.

I heard voices drift from down the hall and a faint clank of metal on metal to my right from the direction of the kitchen.

"Mr. Belew," the receptionist said with a hint of surprise as she replaced the phone, "the Senator is resting from surgery right now and can't be disturbed. Everyone else is waiting in the parlor if you care to join them."

"I'll do that," I said and thanked her.

Yes, there's an actual parlor in the house. There's also a dining room and a library. Every comfort of home is available. The clinically sterile realities of the place are artfully hidden away. Too mundane. Still, there's a faint hospital smell that floats around to remind you of where you really are.

I walked through the door behind her desk and began the trek to the parlor. Every few feet there was a small lamp mounted to the wall marking my path with soft, muted light. Again I heard voices and followed them to the end of the hall.

My trip ended in front of another foreboding door. Two doors, actually. Two four-foot-wide-by-ten-foot-tall sliding, walnut panels, delicately balanced on a hidden track. When opened, the doors hide in the walls on each side. Over a hundred years of hands had reached out and parted these doors.

When I think about it now, the doors remind me of shutters in a huge camera, opening up to let in light and forever freeze a split-second scene. A scene to bring warmth to the hearts of genteel societies all across the country. A scene of beautiful people mingling in a beautiful room while sipping from beautiful china cups and crystal glasses. An elbow propped casually on the fireplace mantle; a hand absent-mindedly caressing the fine fabric of a wing-backed chair. Glints of light from the brass lamps captured on surfaces of straight, white teeth. And, here and there, discreet, tasteful glimpses of personal wealth: dime-thin watches, tailored clothing, tight, paid-for faces.

The moment of my arrival was broken by the almost silent shush of the doors sliding open. A roomful of perfect people became quiet and turned to look at me. And they looked. The urge to check my shoes for dog shit was strong but I ignored it and took a step forward, comfortable now with whatever right I had to be there.

Most of my family was in the room but I felt more welcomed by the people I didn't know. Some I recognized as my father's staff, others were familiar to me from television or newspapers. Aunts, uncles, and cousins made note of my presence with slow blinks of surprise, then turned back to their conversations.

The most amazing thing about this situation is that an outsider would never know it was two o'clock in the morning and the patriarch of the family was dying two floors above them. Hair was perfect; makeup expertly applied; clothes seemed to have been carefully chosen for the occasion. It was more like an early evening cocktail party complete with undeserved laughter and mind-numbing chitchat. My family.

"Well, I'll be damned!" A voice oiled its way from the back of the room. "Daddy's baby boy decided to make a showing after all! How generous, Ambrose, for you to make the trip!"

Now you know why I prefer to be called Blue instead of the name I was born with.

"Junior," I said, and nodded at my big brother.

He reddened a bit and gritted his teeth. Junior's the oldest and wanted to be called Austin, just like the old man. Most of his forty-two years have been spent reminding people of that, but I like "Junior" and have always used it as much as possible just to piss him off. I can't help it. He's a lawyer, held in high regard by himself and his wife, who was clinging to his arm and glaring at me while whispering calming words into his ear. Years of self-importance and condescending acceptance from the rest of the family have made him fat, and he looks like a classy version of the Skipper on "Gilligan's Island." Junior's not stupid, he's just not as smart as he thinks he is. His struggle to maintain position and some degree of respect in our father's eyes had been a hard one. Sometimes I almost feel sorry for him. Almost.

I could see some of my family smiling into their drinks over my exchange with Junior. Nobody approached me, though. That's not the way it works. And before I knew it, before I could put a check to it, I found myself following the same protocol of the same people I'd been trying to escape all these years. It was that blood thing again. First, a drink.

The room was packed and I had to shoulder my way to the far left corner, murmuring "How are you?" and "Good to see you again" as I went. The trip was easy; no one wanted to come into contact with me, it seemed, and moved away as much as possible as I passed. I poured some bourbon — no beer here — and eased into Phase Two: pretended indifference. A show of interest in what's going on is not the proper demeanor in situations like this. Boredom or slight amusement are the best poses, so I slipped my left hand into my pocket and looked around the room. I sighed. I sipped my drink. I sighed again and looked around the room some more. Sip . . . sigh . . . look. Sip . . . sigh . . . look.

"I see you haven't lost a taste for good liquor, at least," someone behind me said.

I turned and was greeted by my sister's smile. "There was no Bud," I told Amy. I wanted to hug her but didn't. Instead, we exchanged a "hey."

"Good trip?" she asked.

"S'okay. A lot of rain, though."

She laughed. "I can see that. What did you do, walk home in it?"

Then I did hug her. And she hugged me.

Even in a room full of kin and close family associates our display caused a few whispers. We Belews, from birth, are taught not to act like real people. Firm handshakes and air kisses are the only types of physical contact deemed proper in public. Emotions are left to interpretation from an elevated eyebrow, a slight nod of the head or any variation of a smile. And God help a crying eye.

But I didn't care. Of all the people in my family, or in the world for that matter, Amy's my favorite. She's six years younger than me but is the closest thing to a best friend I've ever had.

As the only daughter, certain things were expected of Amy: to be beautiful, to be smart, and to marry into a family with a fine bloodline. Forever and ever. Amen. Amy's done it all except the marrying, and I pity whoever provides that part of the formula.

"I didn't think you'd come, you asshole," she said and punched me in the shoulder.

I gritted my teeth and hissed. She knew I wouldn't hit her back and had used that knowledge to her advantage for years.

"You knew I would, Amy, if you called. Remember our promise?"

She smiled and I knew she did. Amy's the only one who knows where I've been. When I left, a promise was made to come when called.

"How is he?" I asked.

"He's bad, Blue, real bad. Uncle Armond says he won't last too much longer." Doctor Uncle Armond, my father's brother.

I shook my head. "Do you believe that? You think the old man's gonna let something like this kill him? I don't think so." My father had always carried off the pretense of immortality better than anyone I knew.

Amy poured herself a shot and a half of bourbon and drank it. She made a face.

"He's gonna die, Blue," she said, "he's really gonna die."

"Where's Mama?" I asked.

"Upstairs in Daddy's room waiting for him to wake up, I guess."

Her casual response irritated me instantly. "Well, goddam, Amy, is she okay, or what? Is somebody lookin' out for her?"

Amy countered in kind. Slamming her drink on the bar, she said, "What difference does it make to you, little Ambrose? It's not like you've been that concerned over family matters these past few years, now is it? You know how Mama is anyway."

She was right, I did know how Mama was.

"I'm sorry," I said. "It was a weird trip and I'm worn out. Let's talk later. I'm goin' upstairs."

"That's okay," she said and hugged me again. "I'm just glad you're back." She stepped away, with her hands still on my shoulders and looked me in the eye. "You'll have to stay now, Blue. You know that. You'll have to stay."

"No way, Amy. Ain't no way." I turned away from her and pushed through the crowd.

Two of my cousins were eyeing me as I walked across the room. They were sharing the same half-assed smirk and elevated eyebrow. I guess it was some kind of show of superiority. I grinned and flipped them the finger.

Besides the parlor, the first floor also housed the administrative offices. The second floor had an operating room and several labs. My father's room was on the third floor. There was an elevator, but I would have had to face the girl at the desk, so I took the stairs.

Standing halfway up the second flight was my Uncle Armond, the doctor; he was talking to another doctor. The two men seemed to be floating in mid-air, standing on that narrow step, with nothing but the darkness of the ascending staircase behind them. With their white coats, furrowed brows, and half-glasses, they looked to be two minor deities. They stopped talking when I appeared. Uncle Armond motioned the other man down, then stood waiting for me to come up.

Uncle Armond had always been good to me and when I was beside him he took both my hands in his.

"It's been too long, boy," he said. "I ought to kick your ass." He smiled.

"I've been in hiding," I told him, and shrugged. "You know how it is."

He knew everything and nodded his understanding, waiting for the big question.

"So. Is the old man in as bad a shape as I've been told?" I asked.

"Yeah, Blue," he sighed. "The surgery didn't do any good. The cancer's taken over, won't let go. As far as time goes, it's pretty much up to Austin. He's not gonna give up easy."

"I didn't think so," I said. "Is it okay for me to go up and see him?"

Uncle Armond studied my face.

"You should know better about that, Blue, than I do," he said. "He's awake, though, if you want to give it a try." He patted my shoulder. "Come see me when you get a chance."

"I will," I said. "Thanks."

My mother was standing in the hallway of the third floor wearing a blue bathrobe, drinking straight from a bottle of Boodles gin, and talking to the wall. Her hands flew up and fluttered in punctuation to each word she spoke, sloshing gin all over herself in the process.

"And do you know I never once went back to that damned furniture store again? Not once, I tell you! Why, that salesman wouldn't know a chifforobe if one jumped up and bit him on the ass! Now I . . . I know a chifforobe when I see one!" Her right hand went to her head and tried to smooth the halo of white hair floating about her face. She cocked her head a bit as if listening.

"Why, no!" she exclaimed, seemingly appalled. "I never, ever kicked that man! That's a vicious lie that has never been proven!" She leaned into the wall and shielded her lips with her hand. Her whisper was one of conspirator to conspirator. "I'll tell you, though, he squealed like a little girl, that prissy, little man did!" She threw her head back and laughed and laughed.

"Mama," I said. "Mama."

My mother jerked erect and turned to face me. Her eyes closed to slits of accusation and she crossed her arms in defiance.

"I didn't do a thing!" she declared.

"It's me, Mama. Blue. I've come home to see you. How've you been, Mama?"

If anything would have made my homecoming a happier experience, it would've been showing up here and finding her on one of her "good" days. Mama's not crazy. She just has ways of making life more "comfortable." These ways include seeing things exactly the way she wants to see them regardless of the facts. Oh . . . and drinking a lot.

She studied me again and her face lit up.

"Blue!" she yelled. "My little, baby boy!" And she ran to me and grabbed me with a strength belying her bird-like frame.

"Hey, Mama," I said and kissed her on the top of her head. She smelled like gin and baby powder; the most wonderful aroma in the world to me.

She pushed away and looked up at me, beaming. "You've come to see your daddy, haven't you? Oh my goodness, but he'll be so happy to see you! I'll bet you're about to bust wide open just waitin' to go in to talk to him, aren't you?"

Mama never saw the need to acknowledge what went on between my old man and me. Just part of how she kept her world in control.

"Yeah, Mama, you're right. I can't wait," I lied. "But you need to get somebody to take you home now. You get some rest 'cause I know you've been helpin' out here all day." I hugged her tight again. "I'll see you after while and we'll catch up on things."

"Alright, baby," she said, patting me on the face. "I'm so happy you're back. So happy. You go on in and see your daddy now." She kissed me on the cheek and walked down the hall.

My father's room turned out to be the same one old Uncle Ames had spent his last days in. A nurse came out as I stood waiting for my courage to grow.

"Is he awake?" I asked her.

She nodded yes, then asked who I was.

"I'm his son," I told her. "Can I go in?"

She was a guard, in a way, and my father was her charge. I could tell she wasn't going to take my request lightly and her assessment of me was my ticket in.

Something told her I was okay.

In the space of an hour I'd grown to hate doors. Or maybe it's been a life-long thing, this door phobia. I didn't want to touch the one before me now, scared of what was on the other side, but I reached out and pushed it open.

No déjà vu. The big wooden bed had been replaced with the standard hospital type — one with rails and an elevating frame. The patterned quilts were gone, too. White blankets and sheets covered the bed now. And the machines had been taken from their hiding places and set about the room. Hisses and whirs and clicks joined in rhythm, singing to the sick. Faint glows of red and green from dials and switches cast feeble light, but enough to see. And beneath the starched linen, looking for all the world like they were made for him and him alone, was my dad.

One hand was on his chest, the other on the bed beside him. He was breathing strong, I could tell, and his signature snow-white hair was swept back from his forehead and arranged neatly on the pillow. His profile, his jaw, was rock hard; clenched tight and stark in the shadows thrown by the machines. I knew he was pissed off at being sick.

As I stood in the doorway, mildly petrified and wondering if I should leave before he noticed me, he turned his face toward mine. And in the voice that made him famous — the voice that made people believe what he wanted them to believe — in a voice unweakened by hours beneath a surgeon's blade, he asked me, "What the fuck are you doin' here?"

Chapter Three

—

I SUPPOSE I COULD'VE BEEN SYMPATHETIC AND TOLD MYSELF his greeting was a result of his illness or postoperative stress, that he didn't know what he was saying. But it was him, alright. If I was surprised by anything, it was that he didn't leap out of bed, grab me by the hair, and throw my ass out the front door. Too many stitches, I guess.

And the most unsettling thing of all, besides finding out he was indeed disabled, was how, for a few seconds, I had a vision of myself lying in that bed. We look that much alike, my dad and I. Of course, my hair is a dark, reddish-blond, not white, but it's the same length and we have the same widow's peak. We share bone structure and noses, too. Both sharp and angular; good for casting shadows. And there's no mistaking whose eyes I have. The ice-blue of mine is identical to my old man's. I haven't perfected that blood-freezing gaze like he has, though. Don't want to.

In the days when we were still buddies, the fact that I was almost an identical twin to him seemed to make him proud. His colleagues, the ones who dared speak to him in such terms, could always be counted on to say things like, "Well, we know you were home at least one night, don't we, Austin." Or, "I'll be damned, Austin, that boy's proof you ain't shootin' blanks!" And always, always these statements were followed by a sharp elbow to the ribs and a wink. Most of the time I was left to handle the full force of this embarrassment by myself because the old man was beaming. A big grin acknowledging the compliments to his reproductive abilities. Oh, I liked it, too. Then. I ate it up — amazed at those stogie-smoking senators pushing drinks into my virgin hands and dropping hints around their beauty-queen daughters. The constant prowling around the gene pool was very serious business.

Something happened, though, around the time I finished high school. I began to start thinking for myself. And the thoughts I was having didn't exactly mesh with the old man's. Faking it worked for awhile. But when I realized I was being groomed to one day take his place, I started to buck a little bit. Most fathers would have given their golden boys some time to go wild, time to make mistakes and then welcome them back in a year or two to continue their indoctrination. But most fathers aren't Senator Austin Belew. Nobody bucks him. The war waged between us for the next ten years holds a place now in the Dura Book of Legends. I didn't win it; I just left. Deserted the battlefield. Bloodied but unbowed. And all because my father felt he'd somehow been betrayed by me not fitting my footsteps firmly into his, by not taking my rightful place, as he saw it, in the long line of bad-assed Belews. That's it — the whole reason we think we hate each other.

"I asked what the fuck are you doin' here."

I jumped.

Senator Austin Belew, father to me and one-time defender of the free world, seemed to have lost interest and was once again staring at the ceiling.

I swallowed, surprised at the dryness of my throat.

"Just thought I'd come down and see what all the fuss was about," I said and cringed mentally at the unintended, smart-assed tone. The connection between my vocal cords and my brain has never really been that strong.

"Why?" he asked.

What a question. A whole collection of snappy answers flew through my head, only to be discarded. Then I had it, a safe, comfortable comeback: "I don't know," I said.

The old man smiled, I think, though I couldn't really tell in the green-tinged darkness. If it was a smile, though, it wasn't one of welcome. Nor was it one of those tiny smiles people give when acknowledging all the weird twists and turns their lives have taken. No, I think if he smiled, and I'm still not sure, it was a smile of rabid satisfaction. A smile that crinkled the skin around his eyes and showed only a bit of his teeth. A smug smile. The type of smile a man gets on his face when he's getting his ass beat in a fight and he knows his last defense, a hard kick to his opponent's balls, is going to land dead, solid perfect.

"Get out," he said.

My three years of thinking maybe, just maybe, time and distance would make a difference in our relationship were shot all to hell. I began to stammer.

"Dad . . . I . . . All I wanted . . ."

"Get . . . out," he commanded.

So I did.

Mama was gone and I was glad. I hoped someone had taken her home to bed.

One of the good things about this place was being able to come and go undetected if you knew your way around. The last thing I heard when I sneaked out the side door on the first floor was the faint babble of voices coming from the parlor.

When I got to my car, I took a deep breath and released it, clearing my lungs of bad air. Then my legs began to shake. It was like when you're driving down the road doing everything right and obeying all the rules and a child suddenly runs out in front of you. And because of your skills behind a wheel, or because of guidance from some unseen hand, you miss the child. After the cursing and the self-congratulations, maybe a block later, your chest tightens and you can't breathe. When you pull over your legs begin to shake. At that moment you realize everything you've ever known could've changed, been worth nothing, only a few seconds before. I waited until my near-miss feeling passed, started the car, and drove down Ambrosia Road.

Nothing had changed. The road ended at the massive wrought-iron gates protecting the Belews from outsiders. Or maybe it's the other way around. On either side of the gates were stone columns topped with miniature versions of the statue on the town square. Recessed into the column on the left was a four-inch-by-four-inch metal keypad. I rolled my window down and pointed a finger at the first number of a six-digit sequence. Then I paused, stung by the power of habit. This wasn't my house anymore. My rights to shelter beyond this gate disappeared three years ago. Reflex had brought me to the end of this road. But I was as tired as I'd ever been and willing to cheat a little on my convictions. There wasn't even enough energy for surprise when the gates hummed open at my personal coded command.

The driveway is a half mile of hand-laid red brick, lined with huge oaks and magnolias. Over a century of Belews have paraded past those trees. Beyond them glimpses of lawn flash past. It's really a vast tract, acres and acres, of meticulously tended "centipede," a vivid green, low-growing, broad-leafed grass. On summer mornings, when the very first rays of sunlight appear and bounce off the dew, the lawn, for a few too brief moments, becomes a silver-green sea. And I remembered, as a kid, wading through it on first-light forages, with bits of grass clinging to my feet like a dusting of tiny jewels. I'd stopped the car, gazing out at the grass, and didn't even realize it. I shook my head and continued down the drive.

As always, when the house appeared around the last bend in the driveway, from behind a thick stand of white pines, dogwoods, and azaleas, I was startled. The house loomed and rambled and waited. It was three stories and four wings of history, fronted by white columns four big men together could not reach around.

I drove around back, parked, grabbed the shoulder bag and shaving kit from the seat beside me, and got out.

A light was on in the kitchen and the back door was unlocked, so I knew Miss Emma was awake. As soon as I stepped onto the polished wood floor, I smelled coffee brewing and saw flames flickering in the eyes of the gas stove. An early breakfast would welcome the hospital revelers when the cancer watch wound down. I put my things on the round kitchen island and went to the refrigerator to scrounge for food.

"If you gonna eat, boy, eat right."

I jumped and almost wet my pants.

"Heh, heh. That's what you git, tryin' to sneak 'round my kitchen."

Miss Emma Christmas sat in a dark corner of the kitchen, in a cane-bottomed chair, beside the swinging door to the dining room. She was hidden except for the reflection of light turning her glasses into silver-dollar-sized beams when she turned to face me. I flipped on the overheads and tried to hide a smile.

"Miss Emma, goddammit, you nearly scared me to death! I don't have to put up with this! I'm leaving!"

She stood up, put her hand in her apron pocket, and withdrew a white-tipped, wooden kitchen match. With the nail of her thumb she flicked it afire and lit the hand-rolled cigarette that drooped from the corner of her mouth. With one slow motion, she shook the flame from the match and flipped the bit of wood into a tiny trash can beside her chair.

"You take one step toward that door and I'm gonna smack your jaws like they ain't never been smacked," she said and left a half-inch of ash on the cigarette with one deep drag. The smoke she exhaled was identical in color to her hair. "I ain't so old yet I can't grab you by the nape of your neck and throw you to the floor, either. And I still got my spoon." Again she reached into one of the deep pockets of her apron and this time pulled out an eighteen-inch, scarred and battered wooden mixing spoon.

I covered my head and began to back away.

"You better stop, boy."

She walked toward me with the spoon raised above her head. Her face was stone, without a hint of humor. If I hadn't known her, I would've fled out the back door. When she was three feet away, she stopped and glared at me. Her arm was a blur as she brought the spoon down and rapped me hard on the head.

"That's for runnin' off and leavin' your family," she said and then she smacked me again. "And that's for runnin' off and worryin' me 'bout to death." I made a move to dodge the next blow.

"Don't you move, boy!" she yelled. "I ain't done with you yet!" I obeyed and stood still, taking my punishment. The spoon came down again, striking the exact same spot.

"And that one," she declared, "is for all the thangs you probably done that I don't know 'bout." She checked the spoon for damage then tucked it away.

"Now," she said, "you can hug me."

I took the boney old lady in my arms and squeezed her tight. She patted my back, stepped away, and looked at me. There was kindness in her eyes now.

"Miss Emma," I said, "it was worth facing that spoon just to see you again. How you been?"

"How you been," she mocked and turned toward the stove. I stood waiting for the litany of ailments that grew longer every year. The wait wasn't long.

"The boy wants to know how I been," she said into a steaming pot of grits. "I'm one breath away from dead, you know that, and my feet hurt, just like always, and I think if I have to live through one more day of this heat I gonna lay on the floor and curl up like some damn ol' dog." Another half-inch of ash had grown on the tip of her cigarette and threatened to cascade into the food with every word she spoke. I'd never seen it happen, though.

"Aw, hell, Miss Emma," I said, "you've outlived almost three generations of this family and you'll probably be around to help carry me to the grave."

Miss Emma was born on the Belew estate eighty-seven years before. Her mother and grandmother were born here, too. The first Emma, her great grandmother, was bought off an auction block in Savannah.

"Blue," said Miss Emma, "sometimes I think you ain't got a brain in your head, askin' an old lady how she been.

How you think I been?" She crossed her arms in front of her chest and glared at me.

I knew she was worried about the family; we were all she had. There were no children, except us, and no living relatives. She'd moved into the house sixty-three years ago when my dad was born and had been taking care of him ever since. And she loved him.

"I got to do something 'bout your daddy," she said. "Them doctors don't know as much 'bout cancer as they think they do. If they wait too long the cancer roots gonna get down in the bone and then he'll die. I can't let him die."

For a moment I thought I was going to be the only witness in the world to Miss Emma's tears. I didn't want that. Not now. I crossed the room and opened the china cabinet. Behind the salad plates was a half-full fifth of Jack Daniels.

"Come on, Miss Emma. I can't think of a better occasion to have a drink of your bourbon at five in the morning. Can you?"

She knew I knew and didn't try to protest.

"You so bad, boy. I really am gonna smack your jaws," she said and got two glasses.

We finished the fifth and laughed when the grits began to burn.

Chapter Four

—

I WOKE AT ELEVEN A.M. FEELING LIKE SHIT AND SPRAWLED ON
the floor of my old bedroom. The knot on my head gave
me a vague memory of Miss Emma dragging me up the
stairs with absolutely no finesse and a great lack of concern for my physical well-being. I also recall her cackling
like some crazed housekeeper every time she dropped me.
Neither one of us handles our liquor very well.

My room had not been used for three years. I don't
think it had even been entered. I could feel it. There were
none of those faint traces of energy people leave behind
when they come and go. The room seemed empty and hollow. Only the signs of my frantic plans to flee remained:
half-opened dresser drawers draped with unchosen clothing, the closet door ajar, shirts and socks and books scattered about the floor. All clues to my running away. I was-
n't surprised. I could imagine my father forbidding anyone to acknowledge I'd even lived here. That would
include cleaning up after me.

This was good though, because my head hurt and it
needed fixing. I crawled to the bed, scooted beneath it,
and felt for the slit in the fabric of the box springs and was
slightly amazed to find the little wooden box of fine,
South Georgia swamp weed still hidden and undisturbed.

Another clue as to how desperate I was to leave.

I sat cross-legged on the floor and rolled a joint. A big one. As I smoked, besides the pain in my head disappearing, I began to realize I'd made a mistake in coming back. I should've waited until the old man was dead and then made a brief showing at the funeral. An etiquette thing. No one would really even expect me to show up.

So, high and hung over, I made a decision to just up and leave.

My bags were at the door and I stuffed the dope into a side pocket. There was plenty of space left, so I looked around the room to see if there might be something I couldn't live without. On the floor, beneath the window, was a balled-up, purple t-shirt. One of my favorites I couldn't believe I'd left behind. It was printed with one of the more sensible rules of living: IF IT SMELLS GOOD, EAT IT. I picked it up and shook the dust out.

As I was taking what I was sure to be one last look around the room, I heard the unmistakable hiss of air brakes being applied. Faint, but unmistakable.

I shouldered my bag, waved goodbye to the room, and walked out into the hallway. It was lined with closed doors, behind which I imagined snoring relatives sleeping away the efforts of last nights posturing. When I reached the top of the stairs, I heard the doorbell ring and Miss Emma's footsteps as she went to answer. Somebody else come to shed pretended tears at the old man's impending death, I supposed.

"Oh Lord!" I heard Miss Emma yell. "What's that thang you got in my front yard? Get on outta here, now, we don't need nothin' like that 'round this place! Go on!"

Miss Emma was not easily agitated and I couldn't imagine what had caused such great excitement. I paused before descending, waiting for the visitor to go away.

Another voice. And I froze.

"Hey there, young lady! I'm Sam Lawrence! Reverend Sam Lawrence! Now if ya' think back a little bit you'll remember me from the Dura County Country Days bobby-cue about five years ago! I was a guest of the Senator's! And if ya' don't mind, ma'am, I've got to say ya' still look as purty as ya' did back then! Now, where's the Senator? I think he'd want t'see me!"

I'd really screwed up. Reverend Sam had landed all because of me. I was the one who planted the seed of an idea in the conniving little bastard's brain. And now here he was, fake hair and all, with an edge of victory to his voice. It was a wasted edge, though, because the old man would never fall for Sam's line of bullshit. The Senator was not sideshow material.

"Senator Belew don't wanna see nobody like you!" Miss Emma yelled. "Now go on and get off this porch and drive on outta here before I call somebody! Go on now!"

She was formidable, but nothing Reverend Sam hadn't dealt with before. He laughed.

"I declare, lady," he crowed, "time ain't changed you a bit! Still just as purty and still just as sharp-tongued as I remember! I sure can see why the Senator keeps you around!"

I was sure Miss Emma was immune to his compliments, but I felt the need to rescue the household, since I had put it in scam's way.

Miss Emma was blocking the doorway but had not reached for her spoon: I think she was mesmerized by Sam. He was wearing a sunshine-yellow jumpsuit trimmed with green sequins. His flaming red hair looked to be freshly waxed and puffed. My stomach lurched and my eyes hurt from the combination of his hair and clothing. I slipped my shades on and cleared my throat. The couple at the door paused in their evaluation of each other to turn and look at me.

I could tell Miss Emma was somewhat dazzled. "Looka here, Blue, we got us a uninvited visitor this mornin'!" she said. "Say his name is Reverend!"

Reverend Sam kept his grin and extended his hand.

"How you, boy?" he asked. "It sure is good to see ya' again, even if ya' don't look no better than ya' did last night. Them sunglasses glued to your head or somethin'?"

He leaned toward Miss Emma and spoke from the side of his mouth in a loud stage whisper.

"I think this boy has some kinda' drankin' or pill problem." He gave a "what-can-you-do-about-today's-young-people" shake of his head. Miss Emma responded with a "I-don't-know-but-ain't-it-a-shame" arch of her eyebrows.

"I've already met this man, Miss Emma," I said "and I don't think he's somebody we'd want to have around at a time like this." I shoved past Sam and pointed out at the Silver Eagle bus growling in the driveway. "Did he tell you who's on that bus, Miss Emma, and what he does with 'em? Did he?"

The Reverend hung his head while I told about the sideshow and the money and how I suspected those sick old people were treated. I told, too, about how I figured Sam was here to recruit the old man, sort of like a headliner for his act. When I finished, I stepped aside and waited for Miss Emma to smack the hell out of the red-headed midget on our front porch.

But instead she was crying and sniveling into a crumpled up Kleenex retrieved from her apron pocket. She reached out, arms opened wide, and swept Reverend Sam off the floor. He struggled a bit and his face began to match the color of his hair. Miss Emma released him but stooped over and took his face in both her hands.

"I swear," she sniffed, "that's just 'bout the nicest thing I ever hearda anybody doin'! You takin' care of those poor, ol' sick people while takin' 'em to the Lord! You a mighty special man, Reverend Sam!" She hugged him again.

"Why, I thank you, Miss Emma," he said as he cut his eyes in my direction. "And ya' know somethin'? It takes a mighty special lady, one raised in the arms of Jesus, to appreciate my callin'."

Miss Emma tittered and fluttered a bit and my jaw dropped to my chest. Right before my eyes the second toughest human being I'd ever known had been given, then blinded by, a massive load of Savin' Sam's bullshit. Before I could say anything, she had Sam by the arm and was dragging him through the door.

"You reckon them people's hawngry?" I heard her ask. "If they be, I got biscuits and a whole pot of grits in the kitchen. They welcome to 'em."

"Now, lady, ya' don't need t' put y'self out for us," Sam turned to look at me over his shoulder and smiled an oily smile. "We don't wanna be a bother to nobody, but I'm just tryin' to figger out why in the world I'd wanna turn down probably some a the best cookin' in Georgia!" Miss Emma giggled and I wanted to vomit. Instead, I got my bag and went out the backdoor to my car. It was past time to leave.

As I drove around the corner of the house, I saw Sam ushering Miss Emma onto the bus. He grinned and waved. I ignored him.

Chapter Five

—

THERE'S NOT MUCH TO DO IN DURA, EVEN IF YOUR FAMILY does own the whole town, but I did want to take a quick tour in case I never came back. Just for old times' sake.

It was lunchtime at the Tattooed Rooster Bar and Grill and I knew Elmo, the owner, would be holding court and forcing unwanted advice on whoever came through the door. I wanted to see him. He was my friend.

The Tattooed Rooster is fronted by brick, plate glass and double, wood-framed screen doors, which squealed horribly when I entered the building. It was dim inside and very cool. There was no air-conditioning, but the twenty or so long-bladed ceiling fans made a beautiful breeze. The floor and the walls were old, red brick and seemed to capture what little coolness found its way to South Georgia in August.

Above the fans, hidden in darkness, was a nightmare of huge, wooden beams as big around as a fat man's body. These beams were supported, every twelve feet or so, by other beams, just as big, embedded in the floor. A hand-hewn forest. I don't think anybody really knows how big the Tattooed Rooster is, but the main room looms one hundred feet by sixty feet and served, many years ago, as a grain warehouse. Along the left wall is a bar of hand-carved mahogany. The right wall is claimed by large booths, upholstered in leather. The kind of booths where things are whispered about. Butted up to each beam, on opposite sides, were two, eight-foot, wooden picnic tables, scarred and battered and stained with thirty years of barbecue sauce.

Almost too much to see — a visual overload enhanced by the smells of old wood and cool brick, barbecue and beer, fried pies and fresh-picked, home-grown tomatoes. The final lure, the one that grabbed, was the sound of a hundred different voices with a hundred different stories, the curses from the kitchen, the clink of stainless steel on heavy china, the tinkle of ice. I breathed deep and sighed.

"Blue! Fa' Chrissake, ya' sonofawhore, where ya' been hidin'?" Elmo Flynn's voice snapped my head around as if I'd been slapped.

He walked toward me, ignoring customers who called out his name. Well, it was more like he ran toward me because Elmo never did anything slow. Even standing still he seemed to be moving. He was tall and ropy thin and blacker than hell. But his clothes and his apron and his hair were spotless white. And he was a Yankee. Hard core.

He grabbed me and shook me hard.

"Goddam ya', boy," he cawed. "I knew you'd be back when I heard the Senator, that sonofabitch, was finally gonna kick the bucket!" A hundred or more white faces froze then turned to look at us.

Elmo glared back. "Goddam, ya' bastids," he yelled. "Eat! Then get the hell out! People waitin' for those god-dam seats!" They obeyed, not wanting to risk banishment.

I grinned at Elmo. "I'm still amazed these people

haven't kicked your ass out of town," I told him.

"You know why," he said with a wink and a near-evil grin as he dragged me to the far end of the bar. "These bastids wouldn't last a week without my beer or my barbecue. And all the ladies in town would dress in black and go to mourning." Thirty years of rumors had Elmo carrying on with every woman in Dura, from the mayor's wife to the Baptist preacher's twin eighteen-year-old daughters. I never asked him about it, but I believed.

I sat on a bar stool and spun around to face the lunch crowd. A few people acknowledged me with nods or slight waves. Others would catch my eye then bend to whisper to whomever was next to them. But almost everybody had some kind of response to my presence.

There was a "thunk" on the bar and I turned. In front of me was a heavy, glass mug filled with gold and topped with a perfect one-inch head of foam. Elmo crossed his arms and waited. I picked the mug up, held it to the light, and squinted my eyes in scrutiny.

"Looks good," I said, then held the mug beneath my nose and inhaled. I closed my eyes and smiled. Then I tasted. And tasted again.

"Ah, Jesus, Elmo," I said after a third sip of his home-brewed beer, "it's been a long time. Too long."

Elmo cackled.

"This is a brand-new recipe, isn't it?" I asked.

"Ya' goddam right it's brand-new. I call it Little Chicken. And I'm keepin' this batch all to myself. These red-necked bastids around here wouldn't appreciate it anyway." Elmo had a low opinion of almost everybody in the world and, in particular, everybody in his chosen hometown.

I drained the mug and waited for a refill. "So what's

been going on, Elmo?" I asked.

"Same old shit, Blue, same old shit. Half the people in this town still living in the fifties, the other half still got their heads up their asses." He gave me a fresh beer, then pulled one for himself. "You know, most of the assholes 'round here still don't believe I'm black. I've heard some of 'em say I'm really a Seminole Indian. I think it hurts their feelings to see a born and bred Chicago nigger make a good living. But, anyway, biggest thing happen around here since you hauled ass was the King of Dura, His Holiness, your daddy, coming down with the cancer. Be glad you left when you did."

Elmo wasn't scared of anybody. He'd proven that thirty years ago when he strutted into town holding the title to the empty building that now housed the Tattooed Rooster. His granddaddy, who won the building in a game of craps from my great uncle Sonny, left it to him. Elmo opened for business. And stayed open in spite of attention from the Klan and, worse, the wrath of my old man, who owned everything else in town. Eventually, though, to their credit, the townspeople decided Elmo's African heritage was easy to overlook in light of his barbecue and home-brewed beer. His finest moment came when the *Atlanta Constitution* ran a full-page spread on his place. Elmo bought five hundred copies, autographed them and made people buy one for three dollars before he'd serve them.

"You gonna hang around fa' awhile, Blue?" he asked me.

I shook my head. "No, man, I'm buggin' out as soon as I finish this beer. I just wanted to come by and see you before I left."

"That quick, huh? I'd think you'd want to stick around

long enough to enjoy the funeral festivities. I hear the ol' bastid's goin' down pretty fast."

"Yeah, he is. I saw him last night," I said. "You can imagine how that reunion went. And the buzzards have already started to gather. Every relative in the country seems to have flown in for leftovers." I told him about the scene at the hospital.

Elmo yelled at a waitress, then darted into the kitchen to turn a slab of ribs. He was back in thirty seconds.

"Those bastids," he spat. "Much as me and your ol' man hate each other, I still think they oughta let him die in peace. I do respect him that much, at least." I would never say it out loud but I secretly suspected there was more than a small amount of respect between Elmo and my dad. Three decades of head-butting makes for fine enemies.

"Yeah, well, I don't think I can handle it, Elmo. Besides, he just may surprise us all and get up and start walking on water or something."

He snorted. "I don't doubt it. But, God, I hope not. I was kind of looking forward to buying up the rest of this shitty little town after he's died. Maybe burn it down or something. Shame, though, that the only other human being in this part of the world even coming close to matching my own brain power is on his way out. I'll have the rest of these country bastids shining my shoes within a week after the Senator's gone." I couldn't be sure but I thought I detected a little bit of sadness in Elmo's tone. It was gone quick enough, though, when he began to bray at his waitresses.

"Sit tight, Blue," he said "I'll be back in a minute." And he scrambled off to take care of business. I turned on my bar stool, drinking beer and smoking cigarettes, entertained by the crowd.

With Elmo's absence a few of the locals became brave enough to come up and offer me condolences. They made me uncomfortable; these old ladies and farmers and business people, taking my hands and looking into my eyes. Too much pity; too much talk about Jesus and His will. And little of it sincere. I should've been happy these people felt I was approachable; that I was far enough removed from the Belew machine to be considered one of them. A failure of sorts. And I heard, "I'm so sorry, Blue," and, "He was a good man," and, "We'll all miss him," so many times I began to feel ill and a little pissed off. They spoke as if he were already dead. They almost seemed glad he had cancer. And lurking behind the near-crying eyes and the soothing voices I could almost detect a tenseness, a pressure, as if when I turned my back to them the entire crowd would collapse in laughter, hooting and pointing in some weird form of celebration. I began to feel sorry for my nearly dead daddy.

The door squealed open and then slammed shut. Every head turned to see Amy strutting between the tables like she owned the place. I glimpsed her big-wheeled Toyota truck through the window; parked half on/half off the sidewalk. The men tried to be discreet and the women were openly cold in their appraisal of Amy's tight jeans, tank top, and tiny, rose tattoo. She wore an Atlanta Braves baseball cap and her hair hung in a thick braid to the middle of her back. She was grinning when she stopped beside me and propped a booted foot on the bar rail.

"Hey, brother," she said and took my beer. It was gone in one smooth, well-practiced movement. "Did you know there's a midget wearin' neon clothes at the hospital talkin' to Daddy right now?" she asked as she wiped her mouth with the back of her hand.

"Yeah. It's my fault, too." I motioned for two more beers and told her my story.

Amy laughed. "He sure is a greasy little sumbitch," she said. "I felt like takin' a shower after he looked at me. I thought about smackin' him upside the head but didn't want to cut myself on his hair."

"Why in the world would the old man want to see Reverend Sam?" I wondered aloud.

Amy shook her head. "Whatever the reason," she said "it's got Mama and the rest of the family flingin' fits out in the hallway. Probably afraid he might change his will. And Miss Emma's guardin' the door to his room with that goddam wooden spoon. It's hilarious, Blue. Let's go watch 'em."

"Uh-uh. I'm leavin' as soon as I finish this beer, and y'all can have Daddy and Reverend Sam and the funeral and whatever comes after all to yourselves." I drained the beer and sat the empty on the bar. "Come see me, sister," I said and stood up to give her a goodbye hug. She stepped away and looked at me like I was a giant scab or something worse.

"You asshole," she said. There was no emotion in her tone, and it hurt a little because she sounded like she was stating fact.

"You're such a pussy," she continued. "You've always been one, runnin' and hidin' and whinin' every time somethin' or somebody threatened your little fucked-up world."

I stared, unable to speak.

"Shit," she said and turned back to the bar. "Go on. Daddy don't need you. Not now. Go on."

Goddam. Mamas and sisters — there's absolutely noth-

ing else in the world like them. Wives can be left behind
and brothers and fathers can be fought or fled. But mamas
and sisters can never be ignored or denied. No matter how
cool or wonderful or right you think you might be, one of
these two strange blood kin is always able to fix situations
where you're left standing red-faced somewhere. And
with no defense. But, being a brother and idiot, I tried.

"I don't think you understand, Amy," I began. "I . . ."

"Aw, fuck you," she said. "I understand everything.
Don't you think I know Daddy's an asshole? And I know
you think he didn't treat you fair. Hell, I'm sure you're
right. But he's still your Daddy, goddammit, and he's
dyin', and if you can't go back to that hospital and tell
him you love him before he's gone, then you're a bigger
asshole than he's ever been." She leaned over the bar and
banged her empty mug on the counter. "Elmo!" she
yelled. "You yankee sonofabitch! I need another beer!" I
looked at the crowd and caught a bunch of guys admiring
Amy's ass.

"Sit down," I hissed. "And shut up. You're making a
fool of yourself."

She'd calmed a bit. "Fuck these people," she said, spinning around on the stool and giving the finger to those
still watching. "Fuck 'em all. It'll give 'em somethin' to
talk about over their microwave burritos tonight."

She was right, of course. There weren't too many people in town who cared much for my family. And, except
for a select few, the feelings were certainly mutual. Us
against them. It hit me, in that moment, what Amy had
been talking about. No matter how far away I ran, no
matter how thin my blood bond was stretched, I was still
part of the clan. I couldn't get away.

Not really.

"Alright," I said.

Amy smiled. "Alright what?"

"Alright I'll try to speak to the old bastard before I go. I'll sit by the bed and hold his scuzzy, old hand for a minute or two. Does that make you happy, sister? Do you feel better knowing I'm going to willingly subject myself to his foul temper? That I'm going to let him run me down one more time?"

"Yeah." She was still smiling.

"If you weren't my sister," I told her, "I'd say you were the biggest bitch I'd ever known."

"Thank you," she said. "Now let's go to the hospital."

I took a deep breath. "I'm ready," I said.

We never made it, though, because just then Mama and Junior burst through the door. One was drunk and the other was flustered. Both babbled something about the old man being gone.

"That midget took your Daddy!" Mama cried. "He and some giant black man just toted him out the door and onto that bus! Oh my God, Blue, they've taken your Daddy!"

—

CHAPTER SIX

MAMA WAS DRESSED IN A BRIGHT-RED, SILK GOWN. SHE WAS raving and her white hair was poofed up on her head. Like some old fairy tale witch, she pointed her finger, cursed, and threw evil eyes at Elmo's morbidly fascinated midday crowd. Junior — a 260-pound, full-grown man — blubbered like a baby. He fell to his knees and covered his face with his hands.

I was embarrassed. Amy was disgusted. Elmo hurried us off to his private office, mostly because we were slowing down the servers.

Elmo took charge. "I swear t'Christ!" he yelled, "if you people ain't one of the most fucked-up families I've ever seen! Junior, you fat bastid, just shut up! Mrs. Belew, you're a fine lady, but, Judas Priest, you're gonna hafta calm down! Here! Have a drink! Blue, godammit, do somethin'!" And then he stomped out of the room and slammed the door. From behind the closed slab of oak I heard a muted, "Eat, godammit, then leave!" We were left staring at each other.

Amy took over for Elmo.

"Sit down, Mama," she said and took my mother by the arm and guided her, as one would a child, to an over-stuffed easy chair. Junior stood in the middle of the room opening and closing his mouth like some giant, fat fish. I handed him a drink and told him to sit.

Amy perched on the arm of Mama's chair. "Okay now, Mama," she said, "you've got to tell me and Blue what all this hell-raisin's about. We can't do a thing 'til we know what's goin' on. It looked like everything was under control when I left Daddy at the hospital." She reached out and tucked a loose strand of white hair back behind Mama's ear.

"I'll tell you what happened!" yelled a fortified Junior. "That goddam dwarf preacher and some pulp-wood nigger came and kidnapped Daddy! Just yanked him right outta his room and threw him on a big ol' country-western bus! They were doin' ninety miles an hour by the time they hit highway 280!" He poured three fingers more of bourbon, gulped it down, and glared at me and Amy, daring disagreement.

"That's right, that's right," moaned Mama. "Junior's tellin' the truth. Your Daddy's been taken away. And him a half step away from dead. Lord a'mighty! I'd be surprised if he's alive right this minute, the way they shook him up goin' out the frontdoor!" She took a deep breath and slumped in the chair.

Amy and I gaped in amazement for a full forty-five seconds, the silence broken only by sobbing from Mama and an occasional slurp or two from Junior. I looked at my baby sister and took a step back in fear of her head exploding. Her face was red and grew redder each time she looked from my mother to Junior and back again. She placed her hands on her hips and leaned forward a bit, a stance familiar to anyone who had ever witnessed my old man chew up and spit out his opponents on the senate floor. Amy began to speak in a whisper.

"Just how in the hell did y'all let somebody come in and take my Daddy — who, by the way, was connected to an eight-hundred pound hospital bed — out of the room when y'all were all standin' in the hallway? What happened to security? Was everybody just standin' around with their thumbs up their asses?" Her voice rose a bit, far from its peak, I knew, and tiny, white spots of fury appeared on her cheeks. Amy was Daddy's only true defender and he her only hero. Amazingly they took care of each other in spite of each having a perfect understanding of the other's vast flaws. Instead of a rose, Amy should've had "Don't Fuck With Daddy" tattooed on her shoulder. And we all knew it.

Like a fool I attempted to break in at this point and maybe dampen the fire a bit. Amy somehow divined my lips moving to speak, and she spun toward me so fast I could swear I heard the tip of her braid crack like a whip. She took a step in my direction and put her index finger a half inch from the end of my nose. Her manicure was magnificent and her fingernail — expertly filed and enameled in cherry red — seemed to me akin to a razor dipped in fresh blood.

"You. Shut. Up." she whispered, punctuating each word with an eighth-of-an-inch movement of her finger toward my nose. Mama and Junior, completely silent for the first time since they entered the building, stared at us, frozen in relief at not being in the line of fire of Amy's wrath.

"You're the reason that little slimy bastard's here in the first place. You told him Daddy was sick . . . and you told him knowin' just what kinda' freak he was." Her eyes widened a bit and her mouth twisted some in disgust. "I bet you told him on purpose, you asshole, just so he'd come here and take Daddy away!" And she drove her fingernail hard into the tip of my nose.

Through my tears I saw Amy whirl toward the others to continue her interrogation and, amazingly, saw Junior stand and hold his hands out in a placating gesture. Amy smacked his arms and bullied him into a corner with the very same fingernail she used on me. I tugged my t-shirt from the waist of my jeans and sopped a drop of blood from the end of my nose. The sting of pain clarified things for me a bit and I sidled toward the door, keeping my eyes on Amy's back. Two beers and forty-five minutes had made too much difference in my life and I'd decided to flee while I could.

Mama moaned, put her hand to her breast, and slumped further in the chair. She closed her eyes and moaned again. Amy ignored her, too busy letting her finger fly to break concentration. Junior had retreated so far into the corner I had trouble distinguishing him from the layers of old calendars and newspaper clippings pasted to the wall.

"Ooooh . . . ," Mama wailed and opened her eyes just a slit to see who was paying attention. I was the only one in her line of sight. Throughout my life I'd fallen for Mama's old "I'm dying, but don't anybody worry about me" routine a thousand times and knew all she wanted was for someone to bring her another drink. Not me . . . not this time. But another moan, followed by a hiccup of a cough, made me wonder if maybe this was for real. Maybe the trauma of having her husband of forty-three years, terminally ill from cancer, snatched away by a tiny, red-headed evangelist dressed in a yellow, sequined jumpsuit was too much for her to handle. My hunger for the door was forgotten as I rushed to her side, fell to my knees, and placed a hand on her forehead. Maybe she wasn't acting.

"Mama!" I cried. "Mama . . . are you alright? Say somethin', Mama!"

Hers eyes fluttered open and she smiled a faint smile.

"Oh, Blue," she said. "My baby boy. I'm so glad you came back." She reached up and stroked my cheek with the back of her hand.

I smiled back, willing strength from my body into hers.

"You just lay still, Mama," I said. "We'll get Uncle Armond over here to take care of you."

Mama withdrew her hand from my face and sighed. "I'll be alright, baby," she said. "But do you think maybe you could get me another drink? Just a little one? This old heart needs kick startin' every once in a while." And then, having placed her order, she closed her eyes and moaned some more.

I felt my cheeks flame red. I'd fallen, one thousand and one times. My last.

"Goddam it!" I yelled as I slammed my hands on the arm of Mama's chair and stood up. "Everybody just shut up!" My anger was such that I decided for once in my life (not counting when I left home) to take control of a situation.

I ran my hands through my hair and took a deep breath, pacing back and forth across the room. Then I stopped and stared at my family, who all seemed to be mesmerized by my actions. My outburst was so out of character with my carefully cultivated cool and groovy image that I think it frightened them.

"Okay," I said, "Amy, get Mama a drink."

"Oh, thank you, darlin'," Mama chirped, no longer in danger of cardiac arrest.

Amy moved stiffly toward the desk and my brother, free at last from his corner, drew himself up and smoothed the lapels of his jacket. He tilted his head and looked sideways at me.

"I need the whole story, Junior. I need to know, first, how y'all managed to lose Daddy. Second, I need to know why you're here and not out on the road following that bus. And, third, and most important, did anybody think to call the law? Did everyone of those eight or nine security people just let this happen? Speak, Junior."

Amy, her face frozen, appeared beside Mama's chair, handed her a glass, then perched again on the armrest.

Junior began to speak.

"Hell, Blue, don't get so mad. It ain't like it's my fault. You know how it is when everybody gets together. The only attention anybody pays is to themselves." I was slightly amazed and even a little proud at my brother's insight but didn't interrupt him. "Miss Emma's gone, too, did you know that? When we all woke up this mornin', she wasn't there to make breakfast. Hell, I'm starvin' to death." He patted his belly. "Anyway, we decided to go on to the hospital in case there'd been some kind of change in Daddy, and when we got there, that damned bus was at the frontdoor. Upstairs you woulda' thought the goddam circus was in town. People yellin' and raisin' hell and Miss Emma standin' in front of Daddy's room wavin' that goddam wooden spoon around." Junior, Amy, and I unconsciously reached up and rubbed our heads, feeling years of phantom bumps and bruises. "She was pissed off, Blue, and you know nobody, you included, can talk to her when she's that way." I nodded in perfect understanding. Miss Emma on a fret-free day was sometimes difficult to deal with; mad, she was a hundred and two pounds of hell.

"I never did think it was right havin' that colored

woman livin' in the house. Why, for years now I've been tryin' to get your Daddy to get rid of her," said Mama, trying to pretend we didn't know she and Miss Emma were best friends. But having been born to a gentleman farmer and a Southern lady, coupled with years of afternoon country club socials, Mama was raised playing the game of never publicly acknowledging the "help." Miss Emma had played along, knowing Mama much better than any of the rest of us.

I directed a frown at her, wasting the effort because she just smiled and crunched a piece of ice.

"So where was the preacher all this time?" I asked.

Amy spoke up. "I already told you he was in there talkin' to Daddy, Blue. He came in while I was still there. That's why I left — I didn't like the way the little bastard was lookin' at me. Daddy acted like he was actually glad to see him. Maybe if I'd stayed, none of this ever woulda' happened." I wanted to assure her none of this was her fault but her face was still a splotchy red and she was flexing her fingers as if preparing for another assault. I love my sister, but I am not crazy.

"That's right, that's right," said Junior. "And five minutes after you left, Amy, that big nigger busted the door open and came out totin' Daddy like he was a baby! The dwarf came out behind 'em, praisin' Jesus and shakin' hands and actin' like he was at a Fourth of July picnic! I've never seen anything like it." He shook his head mournfully and reached for the bourbon.

Somehow I couldn't picture Austin Belew taking a spontaneous joyride with anyone, much less a traveling band of tent evangelists. This was a man who'd calculated every step of his life; every moment. Something wasn't right.

"Was he drugged or something? Maybe asleep?" I

asked.

"Hell no! He was wide awake and laughin'!" shouted Junior. "Five or six of us tried to stop 'em but Daddy said to leave 'em alone. Said he'd be alright. Said he didn't want anybody followin' or nothin'! No police . . . no law at all! Said he was goin' cause he wanted to go and nobody had the right to stop him! Damndest thing I've ever seen!"

Mama rattled the ice in her glass and coughed politely.

"What?" I asked, a little more sharply than I intended.

"Now, Blue, baby," she crooned, "we can't be havin' outsiders knowin' about this mess. What would people say? Why, I bet the ladies at the club would go on about it so much their lips would fall clean off their faces. I don't think my poor ol' heart could take it, with all those old women lookin' at me like they were grinnin' all the time, what with no lips and all."

I was stunned silent for a moment by what was coming from my mother's mouth. The lip thing was dismissed easily enough. But I secretly agreed with her for reasons of my own. We Belews had suffered our share of scandal over the years and I was sick of it. And I had my doubts about how Mama would be able to handle any more negative attention. I turned back to Junior.

"That's it?" I asked, incredulous, though I already knew that a word from the Senator was like a direct command from God as far as Junior was concerned. "You just let 'em leave?"

Junior shuffled his feet and looked down at the floor. "Well. Yeah. They walked down the stairs with Miss Emma covering their backs with that fuckin' — excuse me, Mama — with that spoon. Then out the frontdoor and onto that goddam bus. And somethin' else . . . there was a bunch of old people peepin' out the windows of the bus. Scary lookin' old people." He shuddered at the recollection.

Remembering the sick people who, for whatever reasons, traveled with Reverend Sam was like being slapped full in the face. I recalled the wordless exchange from the evening before with the lady at the truck stop. And I wanted to explain to Junior how wrong it was for him to talk about them that way. I wanted to tell him that somewhere along the way those people had given up on themselves; that their children and wives and husbands were secretly glad they didn't have to deal with once familiar, strong bodies growing pale and weightless, oozing fluids and bruising from the slightest of touches. But I didn't know how. I couldn't explain things to him that I was just barely beginning to figure out myself.

The old man didn't matter anymore. Besides, I was convinced after hearing Junior's story that my dad was a willful participant in whatever the Reverend's game was. He couldn't control his body anymore; he couldn't control the cancer; but he could mess with our heads. He could laugh as he sped down the highway picturing all of us stumbling around, falling on our asses, trying to cope with his disappearance. That part pissed me off, because we were doing exactly what he expected of us. But worst of all was the thought of my old man and Reverend Sam pooling their powers of persuasion and using them against those people who had nowhere else to go. Hell, I was scared of both of them and I was healthy.

"See what you did, Blue? That crazy man's gonna have daddy dancin' around somewhere in a tent, speakin' in tongues or rollin' in the sawdust, whatever they do, and it's your fault." Amy had begun to sniffle a bit and rub her eyes with the heels of her hands. Her emotions were never mild and I knew in a moment there would be a flood unless something turned her around.

"What's she talkin' about? What do you have to do with Daddy leavin', Blue?" Junior was suspicious. And more than a little eager to find someone to fault with a situation he had no control over.

Once again I told of how I'd run into Reverend Sam the night before and what I knew of his enterprise. When I got to the part about how all the sick people signed their finances over to the preacher, Junior visibly slumped and his face paled. Then I told him how, pretty much against my will, I'd revealed the old man's condition. How the reverend was able to pluck information from thin air; pauses, eyebrow lifts, furtive glances — all were clues, hints, for this modern-day snake-oil man. And then I apologized.

"I'm sorry," I said. "I didn't know."

"Can he do that?" asked Junior.

"I guess he can," I said, shrugging. "It's not exactly ethical but it's legal."

"I . . . I don't mean the preacher," he said, peering intently into his drink, apparently enthralled. "I, uh, mean daddy. Can Daddy just give his money away like that?"

I gaped at him, finally understanding where his concern was. Then I grinned. "Hell, Junior, you're the legal beagle. You know damn good and well that he can cash in those stocks and bonds, sell the property, and clean out the safety deposit boxes. Just liquidate everything, turn it into cash, and throw it out that bus window. Hell, he can pave every road in the country with your inheritance if he wants to," I began to laugh. "And you can't do a damn thing about it!"

Though he tried to avoid doing so, Junior lost it, wasting perfectly good Jack Daniels by slinging his glass against the wall. He stomped and snorted and ranted and raved. I feared for his life when his face turned a mottled vermilion and flecks of foam spewed from the corners of his mouth, but still I laughed. And I damn near died myself, gasping for air, when he finally found his voice to speak.

"God . . . dammit!" he sputtered, running one hand through his hair and banging the wall with the other. Mama was laughing now, too, though she didn't know why.

Junior spun to face me, pointing his finger, trembling. "I coulda' handled the family's money," he said. "I coulda' handled it all, but every time I said something about it Daddy just looked at me like I was some kinda' bug or something. Like I don't know my ass from a hole in the ground when it comes to money!" He was taking small steps toward me, face still red, still trembling. Me still laughing.

"All y'all think I'm an idiot! I know! Just a big fat idiot who drinks alot and kisses Daddy's ass!" I was choking by now, nodding furiously in agreement. Junior drew closer. "Well, I'll tell you all one goddam thing — I ain't as stupid as I look. I'm a lawyer, for God's sake! I handled all the little shit business deals Daddy threw my way . . . like I oughta' be grateful. Even though I knew all the time he could barely look at me without wantin' to throw up. Even though I knew he was secretly pinin' away for you, Blue. Baby boy Blue, the golden boy." He was inches away from me now and my laughter had stopped, cut off by his last words. I was light-headed from lack of air and almost sick from the smell of Junior's sweat and the liquor on his breath.

"Yeah," he said. "I knew he couldn't stand the sight of me. That he wanted you with him all the time." His face loomed in mine and had regained its normal color. There was a gleam of knowing in his eye. He nodded. "All those years, Blue. All those years of puttin' up with that hateful old bastard's snide-assed comments, listening to him and his buddies make jokes behind my back and knowing all he really cared about in this whole wide world was you. But I stayed with him. I stayed with my family." He stabbed himself in the chest with a forefinger. "I . . . I didn't run away." He stepped back and drew himself up, smoothing his hair and straightening his jacket.

"Me?" I began, incredulous, and looked at Mama and Amy for support but was given instead glares from two pairs of ice-blue eyes. Mama was back from wherever her mind takes her. Amy broke her stare and strode over to Junior and patted his back.

"I already told him that, Junior," she said. "The part about runnin' away. But it won't make any difference to him. He'll just take his ass back up North where he can hide. You and I can take care of this." They turned away from me.

The air felt funny and the room became very small as I stood watching Amy and Junior, huddled together, making plans. It was almost as if I couldn't breath and I realized it was the weight of a stare constricting my lungs. Mama was looking at me with a look only mamas are allowed to give. A look that said she was seeing less of me than she had always seen before. Or more than she wanted to see.

I looked back, trying, somehow, to convince her I was the son she'd always known. But she never blinked.

I'd been whipped and didn't even know how or when it happened. I'd arrived in Dura a hero just for coming back, and a few hours later I was standing, shunned by my family, in the back room of a barbecue joint feeling like the biggest asshole in the world.

And then that goddam blood thing began to happen again and I opened my mouth to speak.

"Hey. Hey now. I didn't say I wouldn't help y'all out. I'm just trying to figure out what's going on." My brother and sister had stopped talking and Mama sat down again. "We can't just go running out the door without some kind of a plan. We need to . . . we need . . . ah . . ." I didn't know what we needed but it didn't matter because Elmo burst in cradling a big grease-stained, paper bag in one arm and a Styrofoam ice chest in the other.

"What th' hell's everybody standin' around for?" he cawed. "I swear t'Christ, if I weren't 'round to keep things movin' in this town all you country bastids — not that I mean you, Mrs. Belew — all you country bastids would die of slow motion! Get goin', Blue!" And he shoved the bag and the cooler into my arms.

"Get goin' where, Elmo? I can't leave now," I looked pointedly at my family. "I got business to take care of. And what the hell's this?" I asked, lifting the bag.

Elmo slowly shook his head, disgusted, it seemed at my inability to read his mind.

"I ain't talkin' about leavin' and goin' back North," he said as patiently as possible. "Somebody's got to go after that goddam bus! You've got to go and get your old man back!" I didn't ask how he knew; there's no such thing as privileged information in Dura.

Amy shoved past me, put her fists on her hips, and thrust her face into Elmo's. I was amazed he didn't move an inch and only returned her scowl with one of his own.

"Blue ain't goin' anywhere," she proclaimed. "He's outta this! He has no interest in my daddy or in this family for that matter! If anybody's goin', it's gonna be me!"

Elmo put his hand on Amy's shoulder, shoved her aside, and looked back at me as if he hadn't been interrupted. Amy sputtered in astonishment and Junior's face dropped. I was impressed myself, having never, ever, seen anyone so blatantly dismiss my baby sister.

"Now," said Elmo, "are you goin' or what? You got eight pounds a' ribs in the bag and a case a' beer on ice in the cooler. That oughta' keep you for awhile, at least until you catch up to those crazy-assed evangelists!" He almost exploded when I didn't immediately respond. "Goddam, boy! Don't just stand there actin' like you got some kinda' choice or somethin'!" He gestured toward Amy. "She can't go, she's too goddam mean! And Junior . . . well, he's Junior." Amy visibly shook with rage and Junior made a feeble attempt at protest. Mama had been nodding in agreement since Elmo'd made his entrance.

I studied everybody in the room as they studied me, waiting. Elmo was fidgeting but stopped when I squinted at him.

"What? What, goddammit?" he demanded.

"What do you care, Elmo? Why are you so interested in what happens to my old man?"

He actually seemed a little confused for a moment, then embarrassed, but recovered with a string of profanity, some of which I'd never heard before.

"I don't care a damn thing about that old bastid," he said when he'd finished. "It's just . . . it's just . . . Godammit! You just go get him! That's all you need to worry about! Now get the hell out a' my place! I got a business to run!"

And Elmo stormed out leaving me wondering what had just happened while my left arm began to blister from the heat of the ribs and my right arm grew numb from the iced beer. Mama, Junior, and Amy all stood staring at me. And amazingly there was no argument from any of them. It was as if God Himself had come down to wish me well and slather His blessings all over the search for my old man and Savin' Sam.

"I'll call," I said and walked from the room into the dining area and out to my car carrying a bag of Tatooed Rooster barbecue and a case of Little Chicken beer.

Chapter Seven

—

I HAD A HEADACHE. TOO LITTLE SLEEP, TOO MUCH FAMILY, Elmo's beer, and South Georgia heat. And I noticed, for the first time ever, that my car stunk. The mildew and old food odors knocked on my head, demanding to mingle with the pain, and I wanted to lie down across the front seat and burrow under the garbage. I could hibernate unnoticed right there on Main Street for a week or two until I just faded from everyone's memory.

But the frontdoor of Elmo's banged open and my mother, my sister, and my brother stepped out onto the wooden sidewalk, squinting into the sun. Mama found me and began to wave gaily as if I were Grand Marshal in some parade. Junior mopped sweat from his forehead with a wad of paper napkins, and Amy stood glaring at me with her hands on her hips like all she wanted in the world was to whip my ass.

I grinned to keep from throwing up and waved back at Mama. She nudged Amy with an elbow and pointed at me, trying to get her to wave bye-bye. I don't know if she did, though, because I began to claw through the trash on the floorboard looking for the screwdriver to start my car. Keeping my head down, I inserted the screwdriver into the ignition, tapped the gas twice, paused, tapped the gas again, then gave a sharp twist of my wrist. My old, yellow Pinto emitted a great, hacking cough and a watermelon-sized ball of blue smoke, then began to purr. It never failed.

I still wasn't looking at my family as I backed out into the street. I didn't want to see them anymore for awhile. Or didn't want them to see me. I still haven't figured out if I was pissed off or ashamed or a combination of both, but all I wanted was to leave. On a mission. On a trip back North. It didn't matter. Getting out of town did.

No one had mentioned which way Reverend Sam's bus had gone after the kidnapping, so for no particular reason I took a right off of Highway 280 and headed south on Highway 45. The only thing I noticed as I left Dura behind was another billboard begging me not to be a stranger.

Three miles out, nausea caught up with me and I pulled off the road. I stood beside the car taking deep breaths to keep from throwing up.

I felt sorry for myself and decided I deserved a beer. The cooler Elmo had given me was full of brown, long-necked bottles packed in crushed ice. They weren't labeled and the caps were plain, shiny aluminum. And there were no arrows on those pretty little caps to indicate easy opening. I cursed everyone then. My mother, my father, Elmo, my sister and brother. I cursed myself for not having a bottle opener. Then I cursed the midget preacher and Miss Emma. There was some very complicated, all-encompassing conspiracy to screw up my life, and everyone I knew was in on it. Near tears, I snatched the screwdriver from the seat and began to pry at the cap, moaning and cursing. I was pouting. I was pitiful. And I wanted that beer.

The cap came off with a faint phfft and light-blue,

home-brew "smoke" wafted from the opening. I turned the bottle up and drank hard, praising Elmo for the wonderful person he was all the while. I finished the bottle sitting in my car beside the road.

Refreshed, and once again right with the world, I pulled out onto the blacktop and stepped on the gas. For a few miles I practiced popping tops with the screwdriver as I drove. After two more beers, I settled into a sense of adventure. Hell, I could travel around a few days, drink a lot of beer, smoke some cigarettes, then call the whole thing off. Claim I couldn't catch up with the bus. The damn thing just vanished off the face of the earth, I'd tell them. A nice vacation. A nice relaxing trip.

Once decided, it was easy to lean back and admire the ride. I slipped on my shades and propped my elbow out the window. It was hotter than hell but at least at sixty miles an hour my face stayed dry of sweat, and the odor from my car's interior was snatched away. I switched on the radio and received only static and bits and pieces of midday farm reports. It was okay, though, because between the buzz of the beer and the dark hug of the shades on my face, I was comfortably cocooned. And I drove contented, admiring the fields of soybeans and peanuts and being slightly awed at the giant irrigators crawling along the rows of crops as they threw rainbows across the sky. Occasionally I met trucks or tractors on the road driven by dusty farmers in sweat-stained seed caps who would throw up one hand or nod in greeting.

Up ahead and to my right, a ribbon of red dirt, washboarded by rain and rutted by uncountable slow-crawling farm vehicles, beckoned to me. It was a hazy, almost-not-remembered, comfortably familiar road. I twisted hard on the wheel and banged and rattled around in my car until

I slowed a bit, then came to a stop. On both sides of me were hundred-acre fields of head-high corn, eye-shocking green and splendidly straight; a massive, organic army standing tall for inspection. There was not even a hint of a breeze but still the leaves moved, whispering, telling ancient, sibilant secrets that, somehow, deep within, I already knew. The road was banked by sand and I could see tiny avalanches where herds of deer had crossed from side to side, from one field to the other, as if inspecting the crop — a nibble here, a taste there — waiting for harvest. I felt a tightness in my chest, in my stomach, just short of an ache that felt good, felt right.

I patted the gas and crept further down the road, drinking in the bugs and the dust and the sky and the heat. Just gulping it all up, mending and patching and putting back together a massive book of memories. Pages had been lost or torn in two or scribbled upon. Pages read once, then forgotten.

Suddenly I was twenty-five years younger and two feet shorter and sitting on the passenger side of my Daddy's old Chevy pick-up — his weekend truck, he called it — with my hand out the window, cupping the wind. I could smell faint traces of oil, dusty stuffing from the tattered seat, the tang of chemical insecticide and smoke from unfiltered, Pall-Mall cigarettes. I could hear old bottles clinking on the floorboard and the buzz of the broken speaker as Merle Haggard scratched his way around the eight-track for the thousandth time. I could feel the numbing cold from the bits of ice clinging to the thick blue-green bottle of the six-ounce Coca-Cola clenched between my thighs and the slow crawl of beaded sweat on the nape of my neck. I could taste the Tom's peanut butter crackers fresh-bought from Mr. Bud's market just a mile from where the dirt road began. And turning my head to the left, I could see my Daddy driving, cupping the wind, too, his other arm thrown nonchalantly over the wheel. He wore a t-shirt and old jeans, and he was squinting through the smoke from the Pall-Mall invading his eyes.

It was Sunday morning, a long, long time ago and we were riding and he was telling me stories. Every time a truck or tractor was spotted, we'd stop and I'd scramble up into the truck bed and dig in the Blue Diamond ice packed in the beat-up aluminum cooler for cold drinks. Then I'd run across the rust-red rows, my feet grabbed at, then reluctantly let go, by the just-turned earth to present my sparkling, burning-cold gifts to the men in the fields, who'd stop their work for a minute and grin at me, then turn and wave at my Daddy. We rode a million miles that day and saw a magnolia tree bigger than any ever seen since. We saw a mummified cow — been there for years, my Daddy said — and, at the edge of the swamp, we stood silent for a moment before clambering in and about the hulk of a wrecked crop duster, wings mysteriously missing, laid claim to by a carpet of kudzu.

I lived it all again. I drove elated, not really remember-ing how I did it, just allowing my senses to take me where they would. I do know I grinned a lot. At the trees over-hanging the road, at the pair of hawks way, way above me surveying their domain, at the way the wheel jerked in my hands every time I hit a rut.

And then tin-roofed shacks — some weathered gray by the sun and others embraced by huge, old pecan trees — flashed by with disturbing regularity. And I glimpsed hard-packed, bare dirt yards, scab-ridden chickens, and, sometimes, dark, dark faces peering from front porches. Some just staring, others stirring the air with funeral-home fans or brushing clouds of gnats away with brown, work-gnarled hands. Sometimes the dusty grays and browns of the houses were relieved by scattered shots of red geraniums planted in blue Maxwell House coffee cans lined up precisely along porch railings.

My fine ride began to end and I kept my eye on the road, remembering that it looped back onto the paved surface of Highway 45. I alternated between minor depression at being reminded of some of the very real facts of life in this part of the world and the gut-dropping joy at the hum of my tires on the blacktop, telling me I could fly wherever I wished.

Coming home was always like that for me — confusing. There were always pleasant surprises. Always letdowns. Like my retreat into childhood a few moments before. The end to the story of that fine, fine ride on that fine, fine day is that it was our last ride; the best one, yeah, but the last one. The old man became a senator a year later and forgot all about that red dirt road. He also forgot how to play.

And remembering was like digging through a box of toys packed away long ago. A box filled to the top with almost liquid memories that you can dip your hands into. The things in that box sparkle with what little bit of magic dust remains and for a few minutes that dust floats in a cloud around your head. And you remember and remember and you play and play. Then you notice that what was once your favorite toy doesn't make as much noise as you recall or go as fast or fly as high. It's a piece of plastic or painted metal. And then it's time to pack it all up again and wave the magic dust away. Play time's over.

I opened another beer and lit a cigarette; chemically easing the pain with the help of Joe Camel and Little

Chicken. I was becoming suspicious, though, that what I was feeling wasn't really pain. Somewhere in the last few miles I had begun to doubt the feelings I had about my family and my life and the way I was raised. I had begun to wonder if my old man was really the son-of-a-bitch I'd made him out to be in the past twenty-five years. Maybe what I was feeling wasn't pain from growing up in what I'd always thought of as a dysfunctional family but disgust with myself for not being part of my family. For running away.

But I shook if off, sucking on my cigarette and the neck of my beer, crawling back into the comfort of believing what I wanted to believe.

The ride had lost its charm, becoming nothing more than one giant, monotonous hum. Afternoon storm clouds began to amass on the horizon like a gang of puffed-up, school-yard bullies, and the heat and humidity hung so thick that everything seemed to be coated with a thin, oily sheen. The cheap Styrofoam cooler Elmo had given me started its inevitable squeak and no amount of shuffling or rearranging put an end to it. I began slowly to go mad. The radio squawked and crackled, creating bumps in the static. I fiddled with the dial and was rewarded with a reedy voice wanting to trade " 'maters and butter beans" for back issues of *Fate* magazine. The lady caller claimed to have seen an alien in her zinnia bed and wanted something for reference.

The deejay gave a tolerant chuckle and in a Southern-fried, broadcasting-school voice asked for her number and assured her one of their listeners would be able to help her.

"And we'll be right back," he intoned "for another segment of South Georgia's longest running community radio trade show after station identification and a brief message from Farmer's Co-op."

Blended voices sang out the call letters. "Double-you, teeee, teeee, aaaitch. Your hometown heart."

I fiddled quickly again with the dial. Wasted effort in a radio wasteland. The only waves directed my way were those of the community trade show.

A stilted, slightly nasal voice questioned me. "Are you tired of being bugged by cabbage moths and striped leaf-hoppers? Are flea beetles making you hopping mad? If you are one of the many home gardeners in our area disgusted with the way these insects are being so liberal with the hard-won fruits of your labor — treating your garden like some gummint, give-away program — come on down to the Co-op. We have in our arsenal a fine selection of hard to find, full-strength, pre-E.P.A. insecticides and pesticides guaranteed to bomb those bugs back to where they belong. And I don't mean bug heaven. It's the right thing to do."

"All riiight," said the deejay. "Y'all go on down to the Co-op, now, and see ol' Lemuel Cobb. He'll take care of all your gardenin' ills. Oooh-kaay. It's a warm ninety-seven degrees here on WTTH with Hoss and another caller. Hey. Jackson, is it? Whatcha got for us today?"

"Uh . . . Hoss? Hoss, I think you're great, man. Me and all the boys down here at Sanitation listen to you every-day, man. You crack us up, man."

" 'Preciate it, Jackson. Now, you wanna trade or you wanna talk?"

"Uh, yeah . . . right. Hoss, I got a pair a' Redwing work boots, size thirteen, I only wore a week. Started pinchin' my feet. I didn't sweat in 'em hardly none. I'd like to trade for a Dale Earnhardt cap or anything, really, that's got the ol' Terminator on it."

"Yeah, boy, Jackson. Ol' Dale showed 'em what it was all about a few weeks ago, now didn't he? Give us a phone number and we'll see what we can . . ."

On and on it went. People trading box springs for baby clothes, country hams for coffee tables. A lady caller informed anyone interested in meeting with other Elvis commemorative plate collectors that they could get together on Wednesday nights at the high school. Give-away kittens . . . house help for hire . . . blood mobile at the post office tomorrow. Hoss handled it all like some great conductor; teasing, taking numbers, paying the bills with homespun commercials. But I couldn't take it and after twenty minutes or more I frantically dug around between the seats trying to find one of my many Creedence tapes. They were all old and scratchy but were fine company. Just as I reached out to shove the tape in, a voice so unlike the others floated from the speakers.

"Hoss? Hoss . . . are you there, sugar?" the voice was old and soft, like barn dust or spiderwebs, and I could almost imagine it wafting up from my dashboard and clinging to the glass.

"Aw, now, Miss Lucy," said Hoss, toning his voice down a bit as if talking to child, "You know I'm always here for you, darlin'. You got a good word for us today?"

Miss Lucy laughed like the tinkling of chimes. "Any word 'bout Jesus is a good word, you bad thing, you. He gave us this beautiful day didn't He? He gave you that gift of talkin' you use so well."

"That He did, Miss Lucy. That He did," said Hoss.

"Well, Hoss, I'm savin' the Scripture for tomorra. Today I want to tell everybody about somethin' special happenin' in our very own town tonight and tomorra

night. We got visitors comin' into Dawson I know everybody'll want to make welcome."

"And who would that be, Miss Lucy? Who's comin' to
town?"

And I knew, somehow I knew, before this sweet, old
lady breathed life into the words.

"Reverend Sam Lawrence is comin' to town, Hoss.
With his choir. And his tent. And all those people to testify. They're settin' up in the back field of the old Tanner
farm. It's gonna be fine, all that singin' and preachin'.
Praise Jesus. You need to let everybody know, Hoss. And
you need to have your bad self there, too."

Hoss chuckled. "I'll try, Miss Lucy. I'll try my best to be
there. The old Tanner farm? Y'all heard it here, folks. Go
on out tonight and support Reverend Sam and his good
work and maybe say a word or two to Miss Lucy. Is that
all you got for us today, hon?"

"That's it, Hoss," she said and giggled like a girl. "Bye-
bye, now. And God bless."

I was about eight miles from Dawson. Eight miles away
from the end of a minor odyssey. A few hours more and
my hands, and my conscience, would be clean. I pictured
approaching my dad, him cursing me and refusing to
leave, then me calling home, breaking the sad news. And
best of all I pictured myself cruising away, free at last. I
could shuck my guilt like a sweat-soaked t-shirt and
throw it out the window.

Thunder boomed and lightning cracked in the swelter-
ing sky, and I lost Hoss and WTTH. I whistled some
weird tune and set my eyes forward, scouting for a place
to ask directions to the Tanner farm.

Up ahead I saw a portable sign advertising plate lunch-
es for $2.99 and oil changes for four times as much.

Below that, in red, plastic letters was MARK FULLER
YOU OWE ME MONEY. I pulled into the dirt-and-grav-
el parking lot and stopped, waiting for the rooster tail of
dust I'd thrown up to settle down. Through the haze I
could see the building was an old farmhouse converted
into a two-pump gas station. One of the pumps still bore
the legend ETHYL. The front porch hosted a collection of
seats: old bus benches, cane-bottomed chairs, up-ended
wooden Coke crates; all occupied. Five seconds before,
the eyes of all the occupants had been directed west,
toward the blue-black clouds. Five seconds later they were
all on me and my canary-yellow Pinto. Eyes hooded by
the bills of seed caps and ringed by dried mud made from
a mixture of sweat and red Georgia earth stirred up by the
tines of combines and plows. They sat before a backdrop
of a once white clapboard wall, plastered now with a col-
lage of multicolored neon and tin and cardboard. Electric
signs extolling the taste of the king of beers were hung
side-by-side with black-and-white notices for long-past
church suppers. Stiff cardboard, cheaply inked in four col-
ors, pitted the benevolent Brody Brothers against the evil
Yankee Dogs in an untimed, tag-team match.
Thermometers and rain gauges and weathervanes, all
courtesy of one Fortune 500 company or another, clung to
every post and on top of the roof. The men on the porch
sipped from soft drink or beer bottles, smoked cigarettes
or spat streams of tobacco through pursed lips. And
looked at me.

I got out of the car and stretched, pretending indifference at their scrutiny. The wind kicked up a bit as I
walked up to the porch and climbed the old, wooden
steps. Nodding at my audience, I asked, "How y'all?"

Most of the men nodded back. Others continued staring. One or two responded with an "Awright" or a "Good. 'Bout you?"

The screen door opened with a horrible squeal of springs and I entered the dim interior. An old, metal oscillating fan, atop a five-foot steel post welded to a tire rim, stood in one corner of the room, slowly turning its head from side to side, leaving a wake of gentle rustling. Through a maze of wire racks, product displays, and red antique, Coca-Cola coolers, beaded with condensation and humming in key with the fan, I found my way to the back of the room and a waist-high, wooden counter. The man behind it tilted his head toward me and asked, "Hep ya'?"

I asked for a pack of cigarettes and, if he knew the way, the quickest route to the Tanner farm.

"Which one?" he asked as he tossed my Camel Lights onto the counter. "Old man Tanner's got four boys. All of 'em farmin' around here."

"The old Tanner farm is all I know," I said, remembering Miss Lucy's announcement.

"Oh. You must be talkin' about the revival." He was wearing thick-lensed, black, horn-rimmed glasses that seemed to double his scrutiny of me. I suspect I didn't appear to be the Sunday-to-go-meeting type to him. "Yeah. Ol' Sam makes his way to these parts ever year or two." And he motioned to a glossy, full-color poster tacked to the wall behind him, next to a display of radiator leak treatment.

Reverend Sam was all shiny and smiling and standing on a stage backed by his twenty-member, blue-robed choir. A shaft of diffused light, seemingly from Heaven, caressed his stormy, red hair and glinted off his postage-stamp-sized teeth. His jumpsuit was green and speckled with sequins and he had his arms thrust up above his head, palms open and outward, his wrists encircled by thick, braided gold chains. He looked like a Christmas tree. Above the photo, in red script, was the heading:

REVEREND SAM LAWRENCE!!
And his
Cancer Casualties for Christ!
Come and allow the TESTIMONIES
of these REPENTANT people to HEAL
your heart and open it to the
GLORY of GOODNESS!!

Below the photo, in black marker, were dates — today's and tomorrow's — and directions.

Sam appeared to be looking out of the picture and directly at me, grinning. I became a little ill with the same feeling I had when I met him at the truck stop. A little dizzy, too, at alternating between wanting to just walk away from the whole thing — again — and wanting to snatch a handful of Sam's hair out of his head.

"I can get you there easier than what it says on the poster."

It took a moment for me to drag my eyes from Sam's when the man behind the counter spoke. I ran my hand over my face. "Pardon?" I asked.

"It's only a few miles from here if you listen to what I tell ya'," he said. "Ya' car might get a little dusty, though. You know anything about driving on dirt roads?"

I left holding a piece of cardboard — ripped from a Budweiser carton — inscribed with a crude map and directions to the farm. Landmarks included two mail boxes, a hog farm, a grove of planted pine, and an abandoned, Sunbeam bread truck — all along dirt roads and all guaranteed to be unmissable.

Screwdriver inserted — discretely, because for some reason I didn't want the porch people to think I didn't have a key — I twisted hard and thought my car exploded. It was lightning, though, followed by thumb-sized drops of rain. I wasted a few minutes wondering whether to wait it out but decided to handle it and pulled out onto the road clutching my map.

Part one was easy: take the next right. I did and creeped along for a half mile or more, sliding through the mud with each pat of the gas, hunched over the wheel and scraping away at the condensation on my windshield. Peering through the rain, I spotted what I thought to be the first mailbox. It could've been anything. According to my diagram, my next turn was fifty feet or so away. The road, though, had become a river created by water sluicing down between the sandy banks. Red-water rapids washing away an acre or two of topsoil. But I turned anyway, determined to continue my mission.

And the rain kept coming, a little out of the ordinary from the normal ten-minute cloud-bursts common to this time of year. This was an honest-to-God storm — steady, hard rain, a little hail, a lot of wind, thunder and lightning. But still I drove, looking for mailbox number two and not paying a bit of attention to the way the road narrowed and became more of a trail with a strip of grass growing down the middle. The rain began to slacken a bit, not from a lessening of the storm but from the canopy of trees over the road creating a tunnel of sorts. I thought then about turning around, retracing my steps, but the banks of the trail towered above me and there wasn't a break on either side. I reached the bottom of a hill, deeply crevassed and thick with sticky, yellow-red mud. The

Pinto inched forward, slipping and spinning and growling, only to slide back at least half as much with every tap
of the gas pedal. I made it to the top, mud-covered and
smelling of brake liner.

The trip down was much easier. Like a kid out of
school, like a big truck with no brakes, the Pinto flew.
Greased with gravity and gooey mud, it flew. Cavorting
and careening. Complete with three-sixty spins. And then
I hit one of those crevasses, a twin to one coming up the
other side, and I flipped. And flipped again.

The last thing I remember was wondering whether or not
I'd passed that other fucking mailbox without seeing it.

Chapter Eight

—

THE DOOR CREAKED OPEN AND A HUGE, HAIRY MAN REACHED in and pulled me from the car. He smelled of bourbon. A lot of it. I pretended to be dead and hoped he would go away, but he tucked me under one arm and began to slog down the muddy road.

My head was bleeding, and every jarring step the giant man took felt like someone was driving a twenty-penny spike into my left eye.

I threw up.

The human bear dropped me to the ground and backed away, frantically inspecting his dove-gray, corduroy jacket for spatters or stains. He checked the leather elbow patches and seemed satisfied until something caught his eye.

"Aw, damn," he said, "the shoes."

Everything had become quiet and the breeze seemed to cease when he spoke and bent to wipe his black, tasseled loafers with a handful of Johnson grass. I forgot my pain for a moment at the sound of his voice. It wasn't a human voice, I thought, it couldn't have been. It sounded more like the earth had opened up and spoken. Or maybe one of the old oak trees in the woods had somehow uttered a word or two. It was as if his words were aged in charcoal and then dipped in liquid copper and amplified through a hollow log before being allowed to pass his lips.

I waited for him to speak again, but my head throbbed and another phantom spike was struck at the exact moment the man turned to look at me. He mistook my pain for fear.

"It's awright, bubba," he intoned, "I'm a poet."

He pulled a white handkerchief from his coat pocket and looked at the blood trickling from the cut on my forehead. He looked at his loafers. I thought I caught a small smile of apology as he bent to resume cleaning his shoes.

I must have passed out because when I opened my eyes he was peering at me, inches away. His head was as big around as the mouth of a five-gallon bucket, and the parts of his face not hidden by snarls of thick, black hair were beat up and scarred. The nose had been broken more than once and the pale remnant of an old knife wound gleamed from the middle of his forehead to the corner of his right eye. It was a face to scare babies.

"You gonna make it, bubba?" he asked. "You awright?"

I nodded, unwilling, yet, to speak and compare my voice with his. He nodded too, as if in understanding and reached into another coat pocket. This time he withdrew a pint-sized, unlabeled liquor bottle, three-quarters full and sealed with an honest-to-God cork. He put the bottle to his mouth, wrapped his teeth around the cork, and pulled. There was a squeak and a thunk and he spit the stopper into his hand. I smelled virgin bourbon and wanted some. The poet drank all but an inch without a pause for breath, stopped to analyze the remains, drank that, too, then tucked the empty away in his coat.

"We save the bottles," he told me, then asked if I could

walk. "'Cause I sure would hate for you throw up on me again." There was a hint of warning in the last statement.

"Yeah, yeah. I can walk, I'm okay," I assured him, able to speak now, having somehow divined he was no threat. "Just help me up."

He grabbed my arm and drew me to my feet. Standing beside him I realized he was at least a head and a half taller than I was. If not for his fine clothes and that fine, fine voice, he could've easily passed for the legendary Sasquatch.

"Thanks for pulling me out," I said and offered my hand. "My name's Blue."

The big, hairy poet grunted in reply, turned away, and began to walk down a trail. I was still weak and dizzy from the crash and unsure of what to do, so I just stood waiting for direction. When my rescuer was thirty yards away, he stopped and looked back at me.

"Well, c'mon, bubba," he yelled. "C'mon!"

I gazed for a moment at my mashed-and-muddy Pinto, ran over and fished for my bag, the barbeque, and three bottles of Little Chicken beer, then followed after the poet.

We walked along the trail for twenty minutes or more before veering left into the woods. The poet crashed his way through the undergrowth and wet leaves, stopping every few minutes to inspect his shoes. I stumbled behind him, grateful for the pauses and the chance to catch my breath. After what seemed like an hour, I saw a light through the rapidly gathering gloom. A few steps later a cabin appeared. It was made of logs and roofed with galvanized tin. There was a covered porch complete with two sleeping dogs who never even twitched at our arrival. A stove pipe protruded from one end wall, spewing smoke.

There was an old sixties-model sunshine-yellow Cadillac convertible parked in front. The door of the cabin was wide open.

The approximately sixteen-feet-by-thirty-feet room we entered was dimly lit by kerosene lamps and smelled of burning wood from the fireplace. It was hot and I began to sweat, fearing I might be about to pass out again. I leaned against a wall where there were three copper containers connected by pipes and coils of copper tubing. One end container sat on a burner fueled by a propane tank. At the other end was a pipe feeding into a glass, gallon-sized jug. The whole contraption rocked and gurgled. Then a clear liquid was spat from the pipe and into the jug.

"Wahoo! Wahoo!" someone shouted. I felt the spikes in my eye again.

To the right of the room, next to the fireplace, was a low, wooden table and two well-sprung easy chairs. In one chair was a man of forty-five years or so wearing jeans and cowboy boots. His t-shirt bore the United States Marine Corp emblem and on his head he wore a beat-up seed cap adorned with a single black-and-white striped feather. Across his knees was a six-string acoustical guitar. A Fender. The man was grinning at the still, happy, it seemed, with the birth of the bourbon.

Hunched in the other chair was an older man, dressed in black. He wore an old leather duster and high-top tennis shoes. His black slacks and black button-down shirt matched the black fedora on his head. On his face were tiny, gold-framed reading spectacles and about his neck was a large silver cross on a long silver chain. Beside his chair leaned a crook-ended walking stick. He was eating sliced bologna and soda crackers. On the table were two bottles of liquor and several cans of potted meat. My stomach wretched at the sight. Stuck a half-inch deep in the center of the table was an eighteen-inch, horn-handled hunting knife.

The poet stomped across the room, ignoring the others, and rummaged through several hundred leather-bound books piled in a corner. He chose one, then flung himself on the daisy-patterned sofa crouched along the back wall. His legs dangled off one end, brushing the floor. I didn't move, scared I might be noticed.

"You sound like some kinda damned ol' hillbilly with that wahoo shit," the old man said to his companion, "You'd think a grown man would have more respect for himself than to be goin' around hollerin' 'wahoo'."

The guitar man grinned some more. "It's tradition," he said and looked at me.

"He's just jealous because he doesn't know his history as well as I do. And I think he's pissed off, too, now that he's beginning to realize I'm a hell of a lot more intelligent than he is. It's only taken him about twenty years." He picked up the guitar, strummed a little bit, and tapped his feet on the wooden floor.

The old man opened a can of potted meat and dug some of the paste out with the hunting knife. He spread it on a cracker and put the whole thing in his mouth. As he chewed, he lifted one of the bottles and took two or three swallows. Then he started the process over again.

"Intelligence is a relative thing," he said as he readied another cracker, "and something I, as a man who knows these things, wouldn't go around braggin' about. In fact, Jesus Himself said 'Be ye not boastful of your intelligence for it is a relative thing.' Would you like a cracker or some bologna?"

His question was directed at me, but before I could answer the poet leaped to his feet and threw his head back. He opened his mouth and howled. I backed up into the safety of the open doorway and cringed. The guitar man grinned wider and the man in black peeled a ring of red plastic off a thick slab of bologna. The dogs on the porch slept on. The howl ended with a low growl and the poet faced his partners.

"I am so goddam tired of you," he thrust a squirrel-sized finger at the old man, "misquotin' quotes. In my poetly existence, I have read and studied the words of all, ALL, the great and famous people in the world. And believe me, Jesus never said what you just claimed He said." As proof he flapped the book in his hand in their faces. It was titled Quotations of the Great and Famous. He glared about the room as if daring disagreement.

"Well, I would've said it if I was Him and He probably did anyway, but there wasn't anybody around at the time to write it down," the old man nodded as he spoke, pleased with his reply. "Besides," he said, "in my preacherly existence I've studied Jesus and concluded that what I think He might've said, or should've said, is not at all out of character with anything He really did say. I wouldn't expect a poet to understand anyway."

The guitar picker strummed some strings and grinned at the preacher. "That all sounds real good to me," he said. "What about you, our bleeding friend, what do you think?"

"It's alright, I guess," I told him, wanting to be diplomatic around these people I'd quickly determined were crazy. The poet looked at me with disgust, flopped back on the sofa, and began reading, pretending we weren't there.

"Uh . . . I wrecked my car," I stuttered, "and, uh, your friend there pulled me out and brought me here. Do you have a phone?"

Before anyone could answer, there was a crash and all three men jumped up and ran to the still. The dogs had sidled in during the discussion and knocked over the glass jug. They were busily lapping up its spilled contents. I've seen grown men close to tears before and there is nothing at all pretty about it. The poet, the preacher, and the guitar picker were all on their knees, gnashing their teeth and cursing the dogs. I thought about leaving, slipping away into the night, but was captured by the sight before me. Several minutes passed before things quieted down a bit. Then they stood, silent, gazing at the floor and mourning.

"Shit," said the guitar picker.

"Shit," said the preacher.

"Yeah," said the poet.

The preacher walked to a darkened corner of the room.

"Well," he said, "I guess we'll just have to tap into some of last year's batch." And he returned from the shadows bearing a five-gallon wooden cask on his shoulder. He approached the table, reverently placed the keg — cork side up — on the scarred surface, chocking it with two cans of potted meat. With ritualistic respect, the three men gathered around and took turns wiggling and loosening the cork from the swollen oak.

"C'mere, friend," the guitar picker said to me without taking his eyes from the barrel. "You have to help if you're gonna partake."

The cork came free on my first try and I held it in my hand, proud, feeling as if I'd just fathered a child.

"Awright, bubba! Awright!" The poet slapped my back in congratulation, tripling the pain in my skull. "That's good luck, bubba! Quick!" he said, forcing my head down toward the opening, "You get first fumes!"

The instant the vapors waltzed up my nose, all the pain disappeared. It was as if I'd inhaled an entire first day of fall or a stormy, summer Sunday afternoon with one breath. And then my hosts produced a clean, porcelain tea cup, patterned with roses and set on a matching saucer. The keg was tilted. The liquid was poured. And I heard what I thought to be crystal wind chimes tinkling way off in the woods somewhere. When the liquor caught the light from the lanterns, for a moment I could swear I saw the glow of a hundred lightning bugs trapped in that stream of amber.

"Here," said the preacher, offering the cup. "Drink."

I did. And everything soon changed. For the better.

The whiskey, born of corn grown in red Georgia clay and purer than any ever offered on a store shelf, mingled with my blood and made friends with my brain. My fingertips tingled and my eyes cleared. My muscles relaxed in relief. I looked at the dogs, fine dogs, and understood them. They were my buddies. The poet, the preacher, and the guitar picker grinned at me. I took another sip. Then another.

I began to speak, raising the cup to the ceiling in punctuation to my wise words. What words? I don't remember, but when I finished my oratory, the poet wept. The preacher said his faith was reaffirmed. And the picker composed a tune in tribute.

I'd always suspected I was a philosopher but now I knew it. My three new friends knew it, too. They closed in on me, wide-eyed and with great respect. For a moment I feared a group hug. Profound people don't like to be touched.

"By God, son," said the picker, grabbing my hand, "I do believe you got it. You were born for this."

"Born for what?" I asked, unable to restrain a grin.

"Why, hell, son," he said, "you know everything. Just like the rest of us!"

The poet and the preacher seemed to agree for they, too, were nodding and grinning while rummaging about for more cups to sample what was in the keg. A round was poured for everybody and we drank and sipped and nodded and grinned basking in the fact that we knew it all. The poet discovered Elmo's bag of barbeque and distributed ribs to everyone, dogs included. I found my way to the sofa and spilled myself into one corner, drunk and exhausted and all aglow with acceptance.

"What is this place?" I asked, indicating the pile of books and the still. For the first time, I noticed a four-foot barnwood plank above the fireplace, wormy and weathered and crudely carved with the legend "We Know Everything." I included it with a wave of my hand.

My new buddies froze, staring at me. The only sounds were a low growl from the other end of the sofa, rising somewhere from deep within the poet, and the steady drip of rain remnants falling from trees overhanging the cabin and pattering upon the tin roof.

"What? . . . What?" I asked, alarmed, preparing myself to run if needed. "What'd I do?"

The fact that the guitar picker was frowning disturbed me more than anything because, up until this point, he'd been the only one in the room who seemed to be always smiling. He took his cap from his head, fiddled with the feather, and cast cryptic glances to his left and to his right, from the preacher to the poet. They sat silent, seemingly waiting for him to speak.

"It's obvious," he said after what seemed like hours, "we've made some kinda mistake in our assessment of you. The fact you have to ask what all this is about means you don't already know." He put his cap back on and looked directly at me. "There are certain rules we've always followed. The first of which is there are no rules. The second being one has to know this before one can follow the first. I'm sad, and a little disappointed, you don't meet the criteria set down by these rules which, by the way, there are none of. You can stay until mornin', though, dry off a little and get some sleep." And he turned away and picked up his guitar, tapping his feet and strumming.

The poet opened his book and slouched at the other end of the sofa. The preacher sliced another thick slab of bologna. Both ignored me as if I'd never even been there. Suddenly I wanted nothing more in the world than for these three crazy people to acknowledge me.

"Wait!" I cried, leaping to my feet. "You can't just invite me in, get me drunk, and praise my speech then tell me I have to leave because I don't understand what's going on! You're breaking your own rules if you do, the rules that don't exist!" I knew my argument was growing more convoluted with every word but, so far, nothing in this place — hell, this whole trip — had been straightforward. "So the fact there is no set of rules to follow means anything I might do or say qualifies me to be here. Right? . . . Right?"

There was an obvious shift in attitude and they all looked at me. The preacher rubbed his chin and squinted his eyes. The picker began to grin again. The poet turned his attention to me, marking his place in the book with his finger.

"That'll work," said the picker, and he tilted the keg

again and invited everyone to another round.

I'd passed some test, it seemed, and was vastly relieved. Why . . . I don't know. But I felt as if any problems I may have had before I got there were somehow made very small and on the verge of vanishing.

The keg was tilted. And tilted again. Everyone settled and I relaxed inside myself, feeling as if my place on the sofa, with that cup in my hand, had arrived — factory direct — with an imprint of my body. Through the open door I could see the dogs turning around and around on the porch before flopping down to dream. Past the porch, in the woods, the cicadas cranked up, providing background noise as full night rolled in among the trees. Inside, the fire popped and the still gurgled and burped. Occasionally, there was the soft slide of paper upon paper as the poet turned a page or the muted scrape of steel on wood when the preacher sliced with his knife. And around, or above, or maybe even beyond it all were new tunes flowing from the fingers of the picker. Tunes in time with the cicadas and the pops and the slides and the scrapes. Tunes I figured I'd probably never hear again, tunes for those moments only. I closed my eyes.

"Now here's a story," I jerked awake when the preacher spoke, knowing, somehow, I'd been asleep only a moment or two.

"I saw ol' Tap Daddy in town today," he continued. "That old boy with the gray hair who picks up trash along the road? And he had a Piggly Wiggly shoppin' cart loaded down with a yellow-and-green plaid Lay-Z-Boy recliner. He was pushin' uphill and that chair was wobblin' and jerkin'. I was scared he was gonna die of a heart attack or maybe get car-killed before he got to where he was goin'." The picker had stopped his music and he and the poet were listening, enthralled, to the story. I was much more amazed as the preacher cut yet another piece of bologna and opened his fourth can of potted meat.

"I didn't even know Tap Daddy had a place to sit," he said before he popped a cracker into his mouth.

The poet scratched his beard. "Well, I guess he does now," he said.

"Maybe he was movin'," said the picker. "Or maybe he was takin' that chair to his mama. She's got to be a hundred years old by now. She deserves a nice chair."

The preacher nodded. "I'll agree with that. I'd like to think of Tap Daddy as the kind of man who takes care of his mama. But I don't think he'd be movin', though. Tap Daddy's not the type to change locations. A man who owns a shoppin' cart . . . now there's somebody who's already where they want to be."

Before that night I would've been terrified by this conversation, but as I took another sip, I found myself as rapt with it as everyone else and worried about Tap Daddy's health and the outcome of his trip with the chair.

"That's a fine story," said the poet, and I murmured in agreement. "But I don't think 'car-killed' is proper phraseology. I know what it means, but you just can't use those two words together, especially hyphenated, to describe somethin'. You are not qualified to create words just to enhance the tellin' of your story . . . as fine a story as it may be. You don't have the trainin' I do and even I, as a poet, wouldn't try to manipulate the English language to the extent of makin' up totally new words."

He was trying to be nice and mannerly, I could tell, but his massive voice, coupled with his formidable appearance, lent an underlying air of threat to every move he made or word he spoke. The preacher appeared to be unconcerned, though, and continued eating with one hand while extracting a flat, silver can of Possum sardines and a bottle of Tabasco sauce from the folds of his easy chair with the other.

And as the poet raved and the preacher ate, I had a feeling I was witness to an oft-danced dance, well-practiced and played out on a nightly basis before an audience of three. Five if you counted the dogs.

"Why, hell," said the preacher, overriding the poet's grammar lesson with all the grace of a brick, "if I spent all a' my time bein' careful as to how I spoke, I'd never be able to drop a word anywhere. What I got to say is too important to be restricted by a buncha' rules written by some old bastard who died three hundred years ago. It's for damned sure whoever wrote 'em never had to contend with you or Tap Daddy or never had to struggle with tryin' to find a decent supplier of ringed bologna." He popped the ring on the sardines and peeled the top back. "For a poet, you sure do worry an awful lot about words."

The poet opened his book with a jerk and held it up, hiding his face. I heard him mutter something about "old" and "fool." The picker sat through the whole exchange gazing out the door as if he were all alone. Conversation ebbed again and we were all left to ourselves to ponder Tap Daddy and his chair. No more drinks were offered, so I took it upon myself to tip the keg, raising a questioning eyebrow at the others. The preacher waggled his cup and the picker declined. The poet read on. As I sat down the picker asked, "What's your story, son?"

"I'm not so sure I have one," I said after a moment. "I'm just looking for someone. Someone who probably doesn't want to be found." I wanted to leave it at that, let it rest. Stories seemed to be important to these three, and I didn't feel I could speak about mine at the level of telling they were used to.

"That's a lie," said the preacher. "Everybody's got a story. But only one, though. It's a long one, but only one. Don't ever let some sonofabitch tell you he's got three or four. That'd be a lie, too. There's nothing worse than some bastard tellin' more than his share." He had slathered the sardines with Tabasco and was eating with his fingers. The dogs, smacked awake by the smell, were gathered at his knees like two small children waiting for treats.

The picker hadn't taken his eyes off of me and the poet was peering in my direction over the top of his book. The weight of their stares was more pressure than I'd felt in a long time. With his hands licked clean and the dogs nosing the sardine can across the floor, the preacher added his eyes to theirs and I began to speak.

It wasn't a seamless telling. I was interrupted time and again by one or the other and prodded to add detail or description. Like how I felt when I got the call from my sister or did I really think my mother was crazy or just confused. Or the color of the rain clouds. Specifics on my old man's condition were needed. Trivial things: the smell of Elmo's, my sister's tattoo, Miss Emma's spoon. They dug and extracted, pulled and plucked. And when I finished I was whipped, wrung out.

But throughout the recounting I could picture being congratulated on such a fine story. It had everything these people seemed to desire: weird characters, drama, a little irony. And I imagined, after we had all decided I'd come to the end of my pursuit, that I'd become a permanent part of the group — setting up residence in the cabin, petting the dogs, perusing the books, bottling bourbon. Hiding in the woods, protected by the pine, was much more appealing than I ever thought it could be. The pensive moment was broken by the sudden harshness of the preacher's voice.

"Why the hell are you still here sittin' on your ass, boy? You shoulda' been a further five miles down the road by now!" The preacher leaned forward in his chair, cleaning his spectacles with the tail of his shirt. He replaced them and glared at me. "You need to go on . . . now. And catch up with them people! You think they gonna wait around for you?"

The poet had abandoned his book during the telling of my story and was nodding in agreement with the preacher. "Yeah, bubba," he said, "you got to go. Hell, if I'd a' known you were in the middle of somethin' like that, I never woulda' pulled you outta your car. I'd a' left you there to find your own way outta these woods."

"The Tanner farm's only a few miles from here. We can take you there," said the picker, who was up and moving about putting trash in a plastic garbage bag.

Seeing the picker move as if he were preparing to leave shook me up quite a bit. "Wait! Wait!" I said, jumping to my feet. "I don't think y'all understand. I'm not going anywhere! I'm staying here!"

"And do what?" asked the preacher. "If you're thinkin' 'bout goin' back into hidin', you can't do it here. None a' us got the time to take care a' you. And you sure don't act like you can do it yourself. You as much as told me that with your story."

I was confused and told them so. "Maybe I misunderstood," I said. "I thought I'd been accepted as part of the group. I thought I was welcomed here."

"Well, you are, boy," said the preacher. "Any time we're here you can make yourself comfortable, prop your feet up . . . drink our liquor. But you got unfinished business. When you're done, come back here and tell us the end of the story. It's a long way from over."

"My part of the story ended before it even started," I said, beginning to get a little upset with their pushiness. "Did any of you hear me? Did any of you understand me when I told about my family? I was fine before I got the call from my sister . . . for three years I'd been fine. I never should of come home."

"Yeah, I think we heard everything you said, son. Even heard some things you didn't tell us." The preacher was standing and filling his pockets with unopened cans of meat and wrapping what remained of the bologna with a wrinkled piece of aluminum foil. "And you wouldn't a' come in the first place if it wasn't your place to come. You wanted to — whether you know it or not — you wanted to." He lifted a half bottle of liquor and inspected it in the light. After a moment he slipped it into an inside coat pocket.

"Look," I said, attempting to stop their movement toward the door, "if I'm going anywhere it'll be back to my life up North . . . back to my job. This whole thing has gotten out of hand. Hell, I'm the only one in the family who doesn't really even give a shit about what happens to the old man. Please, just let me stay here tonight. I'll head out in the morning."

The three shook their heads in unison. "Nope," said the picker, "we can't do that, son. I don't think there's any way we can convince you how important it is for you to finish what you started, but we can kick you outta' here . . . keep you movin'. And you need to be careful about sayin' out loud what you do or do not give a shit about. Bad luck."

There was a tap on my shoulder, and when I turned around the poet shoved my bag into my arms. "I drank one of the beers," he said. "Little Chicken from Elmo's . . . right?"

I only nodded, pretty much stunned mute at the way things had turned around on me. Less than a half hour before, I thought I'd stumbled upon my place in the world, had discovered allies in the great battle against whatever there was to fight out there. Drinking, singing, reading, writing, and philosophizing. Now I was being shuffled out the door like some unwelcome relative. Even the dogs, who had gotten up to wait by the car, were looking back at me, ears up, with expectant looks.

The others weren't waiting. After the fires were out and the place tidied a bit, they brushed past me as I stood there willing myself invisible. I wanted them to forget I'd ever been anywhere around. Maybe they'd leave me.

"Just pull the door to," the preacher yelled as he patted his pockets for keys. "It'll lock on its own."

Breathing deep and taking a long look around as if I'd lived there all my life and would never return, I did as he said, secretly somber as the door clicked closed.

The trunk of the car, as big as a small bedroom, gaped open and the poet removed a large Igloo cooler. I could hear ice rattling as he walked around to the right rear door. He opened it and slid the cooler to the middle of the seat. After inspecting his shoes, he crawled in after it. Even with his bulk and that of the cooler, there remained room for a den of Cub Scouts. With the preacher behind the wheel, the picker riding shotgun, and the dogs between them, I took my cue and entered the car to sit beside the Igloo. I slammed the door.

"Oh, Jesus," breathed the poet. "You shouldn't a' done that, Bubba."

The preacher twisted around in his seat to face me and exploded. "What the hell you doin', boy! This ain't no disposable piece a' Japanese Hyundai shit! Your ass is sittin' in a 1962 El Dorado Cadillac convertible! Original engine! Original interior! Gangster whitewalls! Only 47,000 miles on this fine piece a' American-made machinery! Show some respect, boy, and keep your slammin' to yourself!" He glared for a full thirty seconds then, satisfied I'd taken my ass chewing to heart, faced front and turned the key.

This car didn't just start; it hummed to life. And then the windows sunk down silently and the top lifted from the windshield, folding back to expose the night and the shadowed pine. A breeze washed away the dampness of the day. The headlights bloomed and foretold another fine ride as they bathed a Cadillac-wide trail blanketed by needles from the trees.

The preacher tapped the gas and the car glided away from the cabin like a big, yellow cat.

To my right I heard the poet scrabbling through the ice in the cooler. "Beer?" he asked, offering a blue-and-white can.

I turned and looked at the cabin. Then turned back and looked ahead. I swallowed and my throat clicked dry.

"Yeah," I said, "I'll take a beer."

CHAPTER NINE

—

RIDING IN THE CAR WAS NOT MUCH DIFFERENT FROM RECLIN-
ing on the sofa in the cabin. There was the same back-
and-forth bickering between the poet and the preacher,
with the picker adding a thoughtful aside or two when he
could. And there was the beer, freely dispensed along with
paper napkins to wrap around the cans and keep the pris-
tine interior just that. The dogs stood with their front
paws on the edge of the windshield, tongues flapping and
dripping in anticipation and their tails slapping wildly on
the seat.

The poet seemed to delight in tormenting the preacher
as he crept along with backseat comments on the condition of the trail or the lack of proper driving technique.
"Watch that limb, preach, you don't wanna scrub up
against it, now do ya'?" he'd say. Or . . . " We are expecting to get there before daylight, aren't we?" and wink at
me, then throw his head back and laugh into the sky. The
laugh was always followed by muttered cursing from the
preacher.

I was amazed at how nervous I was becoming at the
prospect of finally facing my father a few minutes and
miles from there. A nervousness I covered with another
beer to fuel a boldness I didn't really feel.

"This is a hell of a twist," I said to no one in particular, "the lost boy . . . the not-so-dutiful son out to rescue the big, brave senator. It won't sit well at all with the old man."

The picker turned around to look at me with a slightly amused set to his face. "What makes you think he needs rescuin'?" he asked. "Sounds like to me he's in the middle of one helluva ride himself."

I was confused and told him so. "If he doesn't need help, then what's all this about?" I asked, waving my arms; indicating the car, the ride to the farm, their presence. "And why did we have to leave the cabin in such a hurry? You're the ones who seem to think he needs savin'."

"Uh-uh, bubba. We never said that. We only said you need to finish what you started." The poet paused to wrap his mouth around the top of a beer can for a deep swallow, then continued. "The only reason we're providin' the ride is because we want to find out how this thing ends up."

"Look," I said, "I know my old man. He's not acting at all like himself. Austin Belew has never done anything without the benefit of a schedule or a watch." Flashes of long, Sunday afternoon rides tried to intrude but I ignored them. "Y'all are crazy if you think he was in his right mind when he took off on that bus. I know he needs help."

The preacher began to laugh. His shoulders shook and he wagged his head. He laughed some more.

"What?" I asked, on the verge of anger.

He pretended to wipe tears of mirth from his eyes, then commanded the dogs to sit so he could see me in the rear-view mirror. "You're actin' like you got a right to expect certain things outta people. You really believe that, don't cha?" He peered at me as if seeing me for the first time. "Well, you are awfully young." He laughed again.

They were all looking at me with different levels of amusement dancing on their faces. Their scrutiny worried and confused me more than I was willing to admit. I realized I'd spent the last few hours being totally thrown off balance every minute or two by these people and was suspicious I had become a source of entertainment for them. I began to feel unconnected, once again afloat. A few hours before, I was sure I'd found a place to be; I had been gathered by like minds. But now . . . now I wasn't so sure. My only defense was silence and another sip of beer.

The picker turned away and the poet pretended interest in his can. But the preacher kept staring, studying, taking his eyes from mine only long enough to check the trail.

"Why, hell, son," he said, "you sure do get pissed off a lot. I'm a lot older'n you and I ain't been pissed off near as much." This declaration jerked forth a loud clearing of the throat from my backseat companion and an outright laugh from the front. Both were quieted abruptly, though, by a glare from the preacher before he continued.

"All I'm sayin'," he said, "is you sure seem to spend a whole bunch a' your time keepin' people pegged . . . forcin' 'em to stay put in the places you think they oughtta be. Makes it easier on you, though, don't it?" He paused for reply but still I pretended not to hear. He nodded knowingly. "Yeah, it's a lot easier pretendin' you're not needed . . . that you don't count. Absolves you a' all sorts a' things. Sure must be nice travelin' around not givin' a shit."

I was tired of knowing looks and wise words. Tired of people thinking they could open my head and peer into

my heart. For the past forty-eight hours I had been ana-
lyzed by family, bar keeps, and dirtroad philosophers. But
what none of them understood was that I was on the
fringe of this picture. The main event was a short trip
down the road. The rest of the circus was miles behind
me, in Dura. I was a bit player thrust out into the spot-
light against his will.

"What do you mean I don't give a shit?" I asked, on the
verge of whining. "I'm here. I started it all, didn't I? Me.
The only one in the whole family who has nothing to gain
by tracking down the old man. He's the one you need to
talk to about not giving a shit."

The preacher shrugged and said, "Oh, so you do care.
Didn't mean to get you all excited, boy. I was just
repeatin' back to you what you told us earlier." He narrowed his eyes a bit and grinned a half-grin. "It's amazin'
all the revelations that start floppin' around once a person
hears his own words comin' outta somebody else's mouth,
ain't it?"

I felt like I should check myself for open wounds. I'd
been cut to pieces, filleted in the backseat of a Cadillac.

Before I could speak, the preacher raised his hand for
silence and brought our slow crawl to a complete stop.
We'd reached the end of the trail and sat unmoving at the
edge of the blacktop. The poet sighed heavily.

"We'll be here all night," he whispered to me.

The preacher leaned forward, draping his body over the
steering wheel and moving his head slowly from side to
side, peering down the darkened road. There was no help
from the cloud-shadowed moon.

And we sat. The picker began to fidget; the first sign of
edginess I'd seen from him. After another minute or more
he coughed and said, "I think it's clear."

The preacher paused in his inspection of the road and laid his eyes on his frontseat companion, who shrunk a bit. "The last time I looked," said the preacher, "there wasn't but one steerin' wheel in this vehicle." He leaned back and a look of mock surprise sprang to his face. "Why, would you just look at this! Just look right here up underneath my hands! By God! It's that one, single steerin' wheel that comes standard in all American-made automobiles! The steerin' wheel that serves as some sort a' badge indicatin' who has control of forward movement or left and right turns of the vehicle!" He faced the picker again. "Please. Please would you look and see if maybe I was mistaken and there is not one, but two, steerin' wheels in this car? One of which is maybe stickin' out a' the glove-box on your, the passenger, side? Oh, please look and let me know." He turned his attention back to the road, slowly moving his head from side to side like some automaton. I could see tension ease from the picker's shoulders. The poet released the lung full of air he'd been holding and began to breathe again.

The coast became clear, apparently, after a few minutes more and we took a right out onto the highway. There was not even a hint of another vehicle for miles in either direction. After the careful, slow crawl along the rutted, needle-covered trail, I braced myself for a bit of speed but, if anything, we went slower on the paved surface. Just beneath the hiss of the tires through what remained of the rain, I could hear the preacher muttering about "hydro-planin'" and "slick spots." The poet somehow caught on to my impatience and cautioned me with a shake of his head and handed me a fresh beer.

So we rode slow, buffeted by warm, moist summer air and entertained by the fact we were on the move. I dozed a bit, I think, lulled by the touch of the night. The radio played old country tunes at a volume to compliment the sounds of the ride. Once the Cadillac was flooded, fast, with light from a car approaching behind us. The preacher raised his hand to blanket the glare in the rearview mirror. But the car passed quickly, leaving a flock of laughter and amiable obscenities to flutter about like nocturnal birds. And I wanted to stay right where I was for a long, long time, not moving a muscle except to lift my face to be patted by the breeze. I wanted to ride to the other side of this never-ending night, cradled like a baby between a leather-paneled door and an Igloo full of beer.

"Almost there, boy."

The preacher's voice was like a sharp rap on my head and I jerked alert like a schoolboy caught napping in class. He flipped the blinker switch to the left and tapped the brakes and maneuvered the Cadillac onto a well-kept, oft-graded dirt road. Fifty yards passed and we turned right onto a field road and into a hundred-acre pasture. I could hear and feel the underside of the car being brushed clean by the stubble of cut wheat. My stomach curled and knotted as I searched wildly beyond the reach of the Caddie's lights for a glimpse of my father. All I could see was an exodus of insects fleeing our approach. The car stopped and the lights went out.

"There's nobody here," I said. "This is the wrong field. We've got to find the right place. Let's go. We've got to go!" I didn't realize it then but I was becoming frantic at the thought of not finding that bus.

The poet reached over and patted my arm. "Calm down, bubba. This is the place. I don't know what's goin' on, but this is the place. You sure we're supposed to be at the Tanner farm?"

"Yeah," I said. "That's what the lady on the radio said
. . . and the man at the store. Where are they?"

The preacher and the picker got out and walked to the
front of the car as if the bus and the tent and my dad
would mysteriously appear. I kept looking, seeing nothing
but the pine forest bordering the field silhouetted against
the dark blue of the night. And then, acres away, I heard
the growl of an engine. Headlights bloomed the size of
dimes and grew closer, bathing us all in the glare. The
vehicle came to within ten feet of us before the engine died
and the lights faded. I heard the squeal and thunk of a
door opening and closing and the sound of footsteps
through the field. I couldn't yet see with my eyes still
recovering from the assault of the headlights, but I really
expected for my old man to be standing there ready to go
home.

"Hey, boys. Y'all a little late." The voice was fine and
old, like a bit of the night itself had spoken. And then I
blinked, and blinked again. An old man in overalls stood
before us with his hands in his pockets, smiling. "I don't
think I'd ever expect any a' y'all to have showed up anyway."

"How ya' doin', Mr. William?" the picker asked, walking up and shaking the old man's hand. "Miz Tanner
doin' okay? The boys?"

The man nodded and rubbed his hand across the top of
his bald head. "Yep. Everybody's fine, I reckon. A little
too much rain the past few days, though. Reckon I might
have to plow a few things under." He nodded at the
preacher who leaned against the hood of the Caddie and
grinned at the poet who was peeing near a rear tire. His
gaze stopped on me and stayed as he continued speaking.
"You boys out for a little ride, are ya'? Good night for it."

"We came for the revival, Mr. William," the preacher said and pulled the half-full bottle of bourbon from his coat pocket, freed the cork, and offered it to Mr. William, who nodded his thanks and took three swallows. "I hear one a' my brethren was supposed to be here tonight, spreadin' the word." He indicated me with a wave of his hand. "This boy's daddy mighta' been with him. You know anything about that?" The picker leaned against the hood and looked off into the night, strumming his guitar.

I was near collapse from anticipation and these people were setting up camp. But I knew of the rituals involved with visiting and didn't dare break etiquette. Mr. William continued to eye me, trying to place my face in his eighty-odd-year-old catalog. He snagged the bottle again as it made its third round and sipped a minute.

"Y'all still growin' your own corn for this?" he asked no one in particular. Three voices rose in denial of knowledge of growing of any sort. "That's what I thought," he said and chuckled. "Yeah. Reverend Sam was here. Didn't stay long. Didn't even set up his tent this year. And no singin', either. He just pranced along the top a' that big ol' bus for an hour or two then passed the plate. Good preachin', though."

I couldn't be quiet anymore. "I knew it!" I burst out. "He's running scared! Sam knows he's going to get caught and knew he'd better get out of town quick!"

Mr. William shook his head. "Naw, son, they didn't act like they was runnin' from anything. It was more like they had things to do and was in a hurry to get 'em done. There's a difference, you know."

I wasn't listening. "Did you see an old sick man? Kind of looks like me? Maybe like he was being held captive or something?"

"Ol' Sam's always got a bunch a' sick people with him. I believe he takes care of 'em . . . or so I've heard," said Mr. William. "Might be some things goin' on there I don't want to know about, but I think I'd rather be travelin' than settin' still if I was sick or maybe dyin'." He took a step or two toward me and handed me the bottle, peering through three feet of Georgia night and into my eyes. "But, no, son, I don't think I recall anybody with Sam actin' like they didn't want to be there."

I took the offered bottle. "How long ago did they leave? Which way did they go?" I asked, beginning to accept the fact my trip had far from ended.

"Two, maybe three hours. Didn't even eat. Must a' been a weeks worth a' food here, too." Mr. William laughed. "Now that was unusual. Never did know a preacher to pass up good eatin'. As to which way they headed, I don't have a clue." He patted my shoulder. "Take care of yourself, son. I hope you find your daddy." He waved at the other three. "You boys behave. And bring me a quart or two when the time's right." He was chuckling as he walked toward his truck.

"Wait a minute, Mr. William, if you would?" the preacher called. Fishing in his pockets, he walked over to me. Some silent message passed from him to the poet and the picker, who came over and stood beside him.

"Looks like we missed him," I said, smiling weakly. "So much for the great rescue, huh?"

"You're doin' fine," the picker told me. "The trail's not that cold. And there ain't but so many directions in the world; just pick one that feels right and follow it." He grinned at me and winked.

The poet patted me on the back. It felt like someone was thumping me with a country ham.

"Hey, bubba," he said, "you're better at this than most people I've met . . . this lookin' for what you're tryin' to find. You got this far, didn't you?" He looked up into the sky and breathed deep. "It's a good place to be, ain't it? Just you don't be hittin' anymore trees, bubba."

It sounded too much like goodbye to me. "Wait a minute . . . wait a minute!" I said. "They can't be all that far down the road! If we leave now we can catch up! Another hour or two! That's all I need!"

The preacher grabbed my arm and put something in my hand, keeping it closed with his. "I ain't much for talkin'," he said and glared at his partners before they could react. "So I'm gonna do this quick. You go on and find your daddy. Tell him how you came to catch up with him . . . he'll appreciate it, whether you believe it or not." He released my hand and I could see the dull gleam of the keys to the Cadillac laying in my palm.

"I can't . . ." I began.

"I want a full tank and clean carpets when you bring her back," he said. "And she don't like goin' no faster than forty." He held his hand up before I could speak. "Hush, now. I ain't got time for this. We got homes and other lives to go to. So happy trails, God bless and all that." He turned away. "Mr. William, can you give us a ride to town?"

I expected surprise from the poet and the picker but they accepted the exchange as if it were the most natural thing in the world for their friend to give a luxury classic automobile to someone he'd met only hours before.

A few stunned moments passed before I realized they'd all scrambled up into the back of the truck and Mr. William had flipped the lights on. I stood in the glare, shading my eyes, as he revved the engine and began to back away. What I wanted to say, what I needed to say, wouldn't . . . couldn't pass my lips. Instead, I waved. Not much to offer in return for all they'd given me, but I waved like hell. And then Mr. William got turned around and drove from the field.

"Remember, boy," I heard the preacher yell as the tail lights winked out behind the border pines, "a full tank!"

And then it was just me and the crickets and a sunshine-yellow Cadillac in the middle of an empty South Georgia wheat field, marveling at the moon. A few lightning bugs blinked on and off and a cool breeze blew. I remembered the words of the poet, about this being a good place to be, and I silently agreed with him and thanked him for the thought.

For a moment it felt as if all the remaining magic in the world had somehow receded south and pooled in this spot.

I opened the driver's door of the Cadillac and crawled behind the wheel. I fully intended to pick a direction and follow it. But I slept instead.

—

CHAPTER TEN

I WOKE SOAKED TO THE BONE AND BLANKETED BY A THICK, early morning fog. Three large, black, fearless crows hopped about on the ground a few feet from the car pecking at last night's debris. Another perched on the windshield frame peering at me with seemingly great amusement. I shifted in the seat and the crow danced about in agitation. When I raised my hand to wipe my face all four burst forth in flight, leaving me fully awake and trying to interpret the ominous mutterings they tossed back at me as they disappeared into the fog.

I got out of the car and stretched. And, oddly, as wet and as cold and as cramped as I was, I felt better than I had in a long, long time. Except for my mouth. Apparently some half-dead, stinking creature had crawled in and cavorted around for awhile as I slept.

The Igloo still sat on the back seat like some stumpy, blue Christmas gift and I flipped the lid, vastly pleased and relieved to see fifteen or so silver cans floating about in the slush of ice and water. The can I grabbed burned cold in my hand, but before I pulled the tab I hesitated. The morning was too fresh, too clean to begin this way. I dropped the can and plunged my cupped hands into the cooler; drinking deep of the cold water and crunching on bits of ice. I washed my face and soaked my head, then stripped off my t-shirt and slopped water on my chest and back — gasping and whooping in joy at the shock of it all. One of the crows flew in low and slow, then vanished again to go report my foolishness to the others.

I patted myself dry with the shirt and pulled a fresh one out of my bag along with a pair of jeans. Once dressed, I leaned on the hood of the Cadillac and sucked on a cigarette, kick-starting my brain. The nicotine prodded and poked my worries awake. I ignored them, though, wanting a few minutes more alone with the morning.

But my worries didn't come back. It was if the fog and the beginnings of the fine day kept them at bay. I was surprisingly hungry, surprising because it had been a long time since I'd felt like eating the first thing in the morning.

So step one had been established: find food. Steps two, three, and so on would become clear when their time came. As for now, I had a car, a little cash, a cooler of beer, and a cause.

I saluted the direction the crows flew, bidding them a silent goodbye, then slid from the hood and behind the wheel.

I found blacktop and took a left, traveling my old friend highway 41 once again. After a mile or more I pulled into a gas station — damn near a twin to the one I'd stopped at the day before — advertising unleaded for a dollar twenty-nine and sausage biscuits for a little less. I filled up on both, marveling at how a little flour and water and Crisco could be blended together to create something as perfect as a biscuit.

A girl of fifteen or so was standing beside the car as I came out of the store, eyeing me and the Caddie both with great suspicion.

"This ain't your car," she said matter-of-factly, crossing her arms over her Garth Brooks t-shirt and thrusting her lower lip out in practiced perfection, daring disagreement.

In this part of the country, one's mode of transportation was as well known as a face or a name, probably more so. I've heard conversations along the lines of: "You know that one-legged boy with the monkey?" asks one. "You mean that boy who drives that blue '68 Chevy with the dented hood?" the other is likely to reply. So it came as no surprise someone would recognize the preacher's Cadillac. I felt a brief flash of guilt as if I'd stolen the car and had just been fingered for the crime.

The girl shifted and thrust a hip out, striking that pose inherent in all teenaged females. "You stole it, din't cha?" There was a hint of admiration and excitement in her voice, as if I were the reincarnation of Jesse James or some other superstar gangster.

"Nope," I said, watching the gleam in her eye fall to a pout of disappointment on her lips. "A friend of mine, a good friend, the preacher, loaned it to me. You can call him if you want. He'll tell you."

She was beginning to lose interest in me, having decided real desperadoes don't offer that much information. "I shoulda known," she said. "Nothin' excitin' ever happens around here." Then the gleam flashed again in her eyes and she leaned toward me and almost whispered, "It almost did though. Somethin' excitin'? Last night? I was waitin' for Daddy to close up when this big ol' bus pulled in for gas."

"Excuse me?" I'd been digging in my pocket for keys, half-listening. She'd caught my attention.

"A big ol' tour bus," she said, "like the one Marty Stuart or Alan Jackson rides on? You know! I almost peed in my pants!" She was gazing off into the distance now, lost in her own private video. "I thought for a minute Randy Travis was gonna get off and go inside to buy a Co-Cola? Like on the commercial? And then I thought maybe he'd come out and tell me they needed a new girl singer, like maybe their old one got sick or somethin'? And he'd give me a jacket and we'd go to Nashville? And I'd meet Reba and she'd want me to sing for her, too?"

I almost hated to, but I interrupted her. "Which way did they go?" I asked, as gently as I could.

Slowly, she turned her eyes to mine. If I hadn't known better I would have sworn she was just awakening.

"What?"

"The bus. Which way did it go?"

She furrowed her brow and blew a stray lock of hair from in front of her eyes, turning her gaze from me to the acres of peanuts across the road, then back again. The shock of being transported from a recording studio in Nashville to a dusty, old gas station in South Georgia was evident on her face. She pointed, though, in the direction I was headed.

"Thank you," I said, getting behind the wheel. "Thank you very much."

As I turned the key she said, "It wasn't Randy Travis."

"I know," I said.

She seemed to want something more. "Just you wait, though," I told her.

She smiled a bit as I drove away.

There were a few moments of me kicking myself for having slept the night away and giving Reverend Sam and my old man a ten-hour or so head start. They could have been five hundred miles away. Somewhere in Florida, maybe, planning a hit on the retirement communities. Or making a run through Alabama, heading into Mississippi. But somehow I knew Sam wouldn't leave "his" people, couldn't leave them. He was territorial. And the more I thought about it, the less worried I became.

Because I knew Sam could no more leave this area behind — this "Deep South" — than . . . than I could. I reeled a bit at this revelation but accepted it. Then let it wash over me; a sort of baptism. It was like sliding my feet into that perfect pair of shoes or like finally scratching that itch in the exact middle of my back. It was a relief to find the reason for the way I'd been feeling the past few days. The feeling just beneath my being pissed off and aggravated. The feeling of belonging down here that I'd been trying not reconcile myself to.

It was easy — allowing myself to become part of this great entity, this vast area of the country I knew in reality to be small. I was just another bit of life flowing along the blacktop veins beneath a skin of kudzu and red clay. My old man and the Reverend were out there, too, part of it all. They wouldn't be hard to find. All I had to do was flow.

And flow I did. From town to town I went, fishing for clues. And though I didn't find any right away, I knew I was on the right track. There was some connection there, an invisible thread that led from me to my old man. It was that blood thing again. And the only difference being this time, as diluted by distance as it was, I'd chosen to acknowledge it.

The towns were separated by stretches of pine vast enough to make a man lonely. Or acre after acre of plowed and planted fields. Sometimes the road, elevated on concrete pylons, cut through square miles of swamp. And I imagined floating above it, witness to everything from horizon to horizon, seeing the towns pulse and throb below me with the rhythm of living.

Passing through the towns was a study in continuity. Though populations differed in size from double digits to several thousand, the people were the same. People I'd never met but had known all my life. The things. The places. I could see it all as I eased through, careful of my speed. The post offices as places for ladies to gather and gossip. The shaded benches in front of the courthouses and government buildings where old men in overalls ruled the world. In every town I saw groups of men propped up around beds of pickups, spitting and sweating, bemoaning seed prices and busted combines. Plump, little local girls, in tight shorts and tans, fanning fires and flirting as they strutted along the sidewalks. I saw the same four-wheel-drives, spattered with mud and spotted with rust, filled with local boys strutting in return. People stepping over or around old dogs basking in doorways. There were lots of rocking chairs and porch swings occupied by lots of people watching me watch them as I passed. People nodding at and acknowledging each other, taking time to speak a word or two.

And I almost laughed aloud at the sentiment of it all. At the simplicity. Because though there were worries — bank notes or bad grades — people still took the time to appreciate a breeze or comment on a fine showing of crepe myrtle. Appointments kept were more like visits and visits were rituals. Only in these small towns.

The cities were suffocating themselves in the name of the "New" South and denying their dusty cousins just a county or two away. I wanted to be mad about it but couldn't. Instead I hoped they never discovered what they were missing.

Somewhere along the way I stopped actively looking for the bus. The need to search had left me and I just drove, reacquainting myself with the things I thought I'd left behind for good.

And like the needle in a compass, the Caddie seemed to take the turns it needed to take. When I was hungry, I stopped and ate, lingering over meals and enjoying myself. That first night I stayed at an eight-room motel advertising air-conditioning and free local calls. The phone book was twenty pages thick and the window unit was broken, but I slept like I'd seldom slept before. The next night was spent in the backseat of the Caddie beneath a tree in a roadside park. There were two concrete picnic benches and a fifty-five-gallon, metal trash can, painted green. A state trooper came by an hour or two after I'd bedded down and shined his light through the window. He tapped on the hood of the car.

"You aw 'ight?" he inquired.

A week before I would have stumbled out with a lie on my lips and a rapid-fire thump in my chest. Reflex. But I calmly told him my name and why I was there. And he listened to me without even asking if I'd been drinking or if he could take a look in the car. He was somehow in on the flow, accepting my story as if he were part of the plan.

"Why, hell," he said, "you a lot closer than you think. They was in Camilla only las' night. Seems they made a big impression, too. That's all people been talkin' about today."

"They put on a good show, huh?" I asked. "A lot of carrying on and such?"

He rubbed his chin. "Naw. Didn't hear nothin' about that. Just people sayin' how good it made 'em feel and all. Good preachin' is all I heard about."

We talked for a few minutes more about the weather and the Braves. As he prepared to leave, he cautioned me to lock my doors.

"Some a' these old boys around here like to shine deer," he said as he began to back out of the park. "You be careful, now."

He didn't even call me "boy."

In Camilla I located the field on the edge of town where Sam had set up. It was empty except for a few flyers and paper cups strewn about the acreage. Parking on the edge and walking out into the middle, I stood for awhile watching June bugs, thousands of them, boil out of the ground to perform beetle acrobatics against the sky. For an hour I did this and considered it time well spent. Then I drove twenty-five miles to Moultrie.

At a convenience store where I stopped for gas and something to eat, there was a poster in the window publicizing Reverend Sam's revival. But gone were the gaudy, four-color placards. They'd been replaced with simple black-and-white lettering on cheap paper, void of photographs. There was a date and an invitation which read: REVEREND SAM LAWRENCE PRESENTS A WORD FROM BROTHER AUSTIN. ALL ARE WELCOME.

I read it twice to make sure, then said aloud, "Somebody's gone crazy."

The guy behind the counter assured me the poster was correct and said his mama had already called him twice raving about the revival.

"I don't much go in for that kinda' stuff," he said. "But Mama sure did like it. I haven't heard her sound that, well . . . peacefullike, I guess you'd call it, in a long time. And if she's happy, I'm happy."

For the first time in two or three days, I became agitated.

All I could think about was what kind of scam was in the works. My old man had never been one to talk religion. Except during reelection campaigns. Then he became the church-goingest human being you ever saw. After the votes were counted, he replaced his faith in Jesus with faith in nobody but himself.

That warm, fuzzy feeling I had vanished and I found myself gritting my teeth and gripping the wheel as I drove. The more I thought about it, the more pissed I became. Not only were the people coming to hear the preaching being scammed, I was, too. I'd actually been having charitable thoughts about my dad. And I knew better. Thinking about him and Sam using the sick folks on the bus to make a buck or two took the game back to the beginning, as far as I was concerned. I'd catch up with him, alright, and then I'd tell him some things that should have been said a long time ago.

The mood lasted until I reached Adel, a town of five thousand or so kept alive, in part, by traffic from I-75. At a fast-food joint, I spotted a twenty-passenger van identical to the one that transported the Reverend's choir. It turned out to be the very same van. I pulled into the parking lot and waited for someone to come out. Fifteen minutes later they all exited. I approached the man who held keys in his hand.

"Pardon me," I said, putting on my most sincere face, "but don't y'all sing in Reverend Sam Lawrence's choir?"

The others had gathered around the van and were preening a bit at being recognized. Their leader unlocked the driver's side door and moved a toothpick from one corner of his mouth to the other, looking at me. He was a tall, thin man with poofed-up hair.

"Yeah," he said, "that's us. Heard us sing, have ya'?"

A lie formed but didn't have time to be uttered.

"At least that was us until last night," the tall man said. "We were let go. Right after the best singin' we ever did and he let us go."

"What for?" I asked. "Why would he do something like that?"

He studied the faces of his fellow choir members and, finding no answer there, shrugged his shoulders. "Nobody knows. Just said as much as he hated going on without us, he didn't need a choir anymore." He shrugged again and opened the van door. "Paid us through the season, though, plus one hell of a bonus, pardon my French. And told us to do what we wanted with the van. Can't ask for any better than that, now can you?"

I couldn't quite picture Reverend Sam giving away money and a car. The image wouldn't form in my brain. The choir members had piled into the van and the tall man had moved to the driver's seat and was revving the engine. I tapped on the window and motioned for him to lower it.

"Doesn't any of this seem kind of strange to you?" I asked. "I mean, you can't have a revival without a choir, can you? What do you suppose has gotten into him?"

He leaned back in the seat and studied me intensely as if trying to divine if I were worthy of what he was about to say.

"I'll tell you," he said, "I've been singin' gospel for a long, long time. Traveled with the best of 'em, too. Brother Bob Scott, the Divine Sisters . . . all of 'em. But Sam, now . . . Sam put 'em all to shame. Sam could talk the horns off a billy goat." He stopped for a moment as if paying silent homage to the master. "To tell you the truth, I was always glad to be in the background. Glad I wasn't at the front of that stage pretending to have some kind of direct line to the Almighty." He leaned toward me a little and lowered his voice. "You know, all of these evangelists aren't exactly on the up and up. Most of it's show business, just like rock 'n' roll." He raised his eyebrows and I nodded appreciatively at being let in on the secret. "Now, I don't claim to be innocent," he continued. "I was one of the bells and whistles, one of the distractions. But that's what I do. Over the years I've come to feel a little guilty about it and this was going to be my last season. But son . . . son the past few days I got the feeling I was part of something special. I was part of the way spreading the word was supposed to be. People are starting to listen. Really listen."

"What's different?" I breathed. "What's Sam doing now?"

He shook his head. "I'll tell you, I don't really think it's Sam that's made the difference. It's the new man he's got with him who's doing most of the talking now. But, you know, I think for the first time in his life ol' Sam's beginning to believe. I think maybe he's falling for his own line and might just start practicing what he preaches." He turned to look at his passengers and laughed a bit. "Now wouldn't that be something?"

I had at least a thousand other questions, but the man had put the van in reverse and was politely waiting for me to step away. "Can you tell me where they are now?" I asked. "Are they far from here?"

He pointed east with his chin as he began to slowly back out of the parking space. "Just keep going that way," he said. "You'll find 'em. It's not like they're trying to hide or anything like that. You take care now."

So I drove east, tugged along by some unidentifiable force. I don't really remember much of the drive except that it was through one of those boundless pine forests. It seemed every few minutes the Caddie was rocked and buffeted by the wind from pulpwood trucks — laden with forty-foot felled trees — barreling and careening along the two-lane county road. My mind was in a static mode, shut down as if resting from all the information and bits and pieces of the puzzle I'd received.

I stopped for gas once at a dilapidated station surrounded by a couple of acres of rusted automobiles and pulpwood machinery. A one-legged man took my money and grunted in reply to my questions while halfheartedly brushing gnats away from his face. I was rewarded with two grunts and a nod when I asked if he'd heard of the revival. And I jumped a bit in alarm when he actually spoke. "Waycross," he grunted, then turned away to watch "Geraldo" on the black-and-white TV on the counter.

Fifteen miles later my heart quit beating. Just as I'd passed a billboard on my right, erected by the Waycross Chamber of Commerce and proclaiming the town to be the gateway to the Okefenokee Swamp, I saw, peeking out above the pine like some limp UFO, a flag of white emblazoned with a bright red cross.

I slowed to a crawl as I saw bits of blue and white flash through the trees. And then there was Sam's tent, crouched like some huge, canvas creature on a plot carved out of the pine and paved with several tons of blinding-white, crushed gravel. There were about thirty vehicles parked haphazardly around the tent, and I pulled in between two flatbed pickup trucks; one loaded with watermelons, the other with sweet corn.

This was not how I'd pictured the reunion with my dad. All the scripts I'd written in my head, all the scenarios, vanished as if they'd never been thought up. I put my fore-head to the steering wheel and sucked in great gulps of air while allowing the blood to return to my brain. And before I could panic, before I talked myself into leaving, I got out of the car and entered the tent.

The light from the South Georgia sun had a hard time penetrating the canvas, but the heat didn't. It was like a physical being that wrapped around me and threatened to force me back out of the opening. I pushed through, though, and stood a moment, allowing my eyes to adjust to the gloom.

Instead of chairs lined up neatly in rows awaiting con-gregation, there were cafeteria tables and sheets of ply-wood laid across sawhorses. And I didn't recognize my dad or Reverend Sam among the three or four dozen peo-ple scattered about.

"C'mon in! C'mon in! They's people behind ya' tryin' t' git through!" Someone grabbed my arm and pulled me to one side.

I shook myself free.

"Sorry, boy. But, dad-jobbit, you was blockin' the way!" The man who'd grabbed me was seventy or so years old and was dressed in a pale-blue, sleeveless jump-suit, splattered and stained with paint. Perched on his head, like the shell of an ancient tortoise, was a bent and battered steel hard hat adorned with layers of peeling decals. He was toothless and grinned at me like a happy, newborn baby.

"You here to buy somethin' or you wanna rent a space?" he asked.

He grabbed my arm again, alarmed at something he saw in my face. "Dad-jobbit, boy, you awright? The heat gittin' to ya'? Here! Siddown!" He guided me to a metal

folding chair and forced me to sit. "You wait right here."
He disappeared and I sat looking at the tables of mer-
chandise being browsed through and picked over by the
flea-market shoppers.

The old man returned and thrust a six-ounce soft drink
bottle, slick with bits of crushed ice, into my hand.

"Drink that dad-jobbed Co-cola, boy!" he commanded. "That'll straighten ya' out! Ain't nothin' like a cold
Co-cola to give ya' a good poke in th' ass!" He cackled
when I looked up at him. "Dad-jobbit! You look as lost
as last year's Easter eggs, boy! You gonna be awright?"

The Coke burned cold down my throat and I sputtered
and coughed before I was able to speak. "Where's Sam?"
I croaked. "And what's going on here?" I waved my hand,
indicating the crowd of shoppers.

"Sam's gone!" he crowed. "Give me this dad-jobbed
tent 'fore he left, too! Can you dad-jobbed believe it? Jus'
up and give it to me! Don't need it no more, he said, and
would I like to have it! Like he even had to dad-job ask!
Why, sure as hell I'd like to have it, I said back to him!"
He stopped his babbling and bounded away to usher an
old lady through the flaps. "You come right on in, Miss
Chumley!" I heard him say. "I believe ol' Tater Flynn's got
a whole truck load a' fresh okrie over in that far corner!
Watch ya' step, now, and you jus' holler if I can help ya'!"

He came back over to me and started to continue his
story, but I stopped him before he began.

"I've been trying to catch up with Sam for awhile," I
told him. "I thought I'd found him when I saw the tent.
Now you're telling me he's gone? And he gave his tent
away? Why would he do something like that?"

"Don't know," the old man chortled, "but I'm glad he
did! See, ever year or so I rent this dad-jobbed space to ol'

Sam so he can hold his meetin's. This year he paid me with cash-dollars and this tent! Soon as that dad-jobbed bus pulled out and I was sure he wasn't comin' back to change his mind, I called up Mama and the boys and told 'em to call up everbody who rents spaces at the flea market down to th' river! Told 'em to tell everbody I got a place for 'em to stay out a' the rain! By seven o'clock this mornin' the place was full! And at twenty dollars a spot! Dad-jobbit! Ain't it somethin'!" He was in full beam now, gazing out over his domain.

I stood up, teetering a bit, and took my first real look at what was going on in the tent. What immediately came to mind was a Middle Eastern bazaar. Just about anything imaginable was for sale, from deep-fried foods to used tires. There were tables laden with cheap t-shirts printed with bumper sticker slogans or confederate flags. One lady dispensed homemade lemonade from gallon jugs.

"Can ya' walk? I told ya' that dad-jobbed Co-cola would do the trick!" The old man appeared genuinely concerned and I thanked him.

"I think I'm going to walk around a bit, if you don't mind," I told him. "Thanks again."

He winked at me. "My pleasure, boy. And dad-jobbit! You watch that heat!" He began to turn away then stopped, extending his hand, palm up. "That'll be fifty cents for the Co-cola! Gotta make a livin'!" And he grinned.

I browsed a bit, breathing in the thick air redolent with the perfume of fried pies and the sweet smell of quartered watermelon. Occasionally I dodged slow-going wasps and yellow jackets drunk from the juices of fresh fruits and vegetables. I bought another Coke and decided to leave. There were two tens and a handful of change in my pocket; all I had. As I paid for my drink, I spied a boy of eighteen or so crouched in a corner of the tent beside a small, chicken-wire cage. In the cage were two raccoons, panting like dogs from the heat. I walked over to him.

"Isn't that illegal?" I asked.

He sneered at me and picked at a sore on his chin. "You some kinda goddam cop or somethin'? You tryin' to start some shit?" He stood and crossed his arms over his chest. His biceps threatened to split his sleeves and the Georgia Bulldog transfer on the front of his shirt bulged and rippled as if alive. At this point not too much impressed me anymore.

"No," I told him, "I just think it's pretty goddam cruel to keep 'em locked up like that. They're almost dead. Somebody ought to kick your ass." I looked him in the eye and he deflated a bit.

"They're just coons," he whined. "Goddam coons. Don't nobody care."

"How much?" I asked.

"What?" He stared at me, slack-jawed.

"They're for sale, aren't they?" I squatted down beside the cage and inspected the listless, rheumy-eyed raccoons. Their fur was dull and matted and they didn't appear to be anywhere near well fed.

The boy had regained some of his bravado. "What chu want with 'em?" he asked. "You gonna put ya' dogs on 'em? That's what I do. Don't feed my dogs for a day or two then throw a coon at 'em. Keeps 'em ready for huntin' season."

"Look," I said. "I don't care what you do with them. Are they for sale or not?"

"Twenty dollars. Both of 'em for twenty dollars. Let ya' have the cage for another five."

I shook my head. "Can't do it," I said. "I'll give you ten."

The boy laughed. "Get the fuck outta here! I ain't givin' you these coons and the cage for ten dollars! You're crazy as hell!"

I didn't know what I was doing. "Wait just a minute," I said. "I'll be right back." And I left the tent and walked out to the Caddie. The top was down and I reached into the backseat and got the Igloo. I knew they were there but I was still slightly amazed to see the fifteen cans of beer floating about in the warm water. The cooler thumped and gurgled as I lugged it back into the tent.

The boy was talking to another teenager when I walked up. They both looked at me and laughed.

"Ten dollars," I said, "this cooler and fifteen beers." I put the Igloo on the floor and flipped the lid. "They're warm but, only a few days old."

His buddy smacked him on the arm and bobbed his head. "All right!" he said.

The deal was made.

I bought an old plastic bowl at one of the tables for twenty-five cents and two hot dogs for a dollar and a half. After I'd put the cage on the frontseat, being careful not to scratch the preacher's upholstery, I filled the bowl with water and broke the hot dogs into pieces and put it all in with the raccoons. They ignored it.

Why'd I do it? Maybe it was because I'd stumbled upon a situation I could do something about. Whatever the reason, it felt good and now I had two traveling companions.

Me and the Caddie and the coons went north, away from the swamps. The top was down and the fresh air put a little life back into the two creatures. After a few minutes they began to pick up pieces of bread and meat and wash them off in the bowl of water before eating them.

"No more. Sorry," I told them after they'd eaten it all and began to peer out at me through the wire. My knowledge of raccoons was pretty thin but they appeared to be very young and mostly tame. I cranked up the radio and sang to them for awhile, then began to laugh like hell for no particular reason. I received quizzical coon looks in return, which made me laugh harder. They had no more idea what was going on than I did.

"Aw, hell," I said and pulled over to the gravel shoulder of the road. The sun was just touching the tops of the pine, pulling some of the heat of the day down with it. There was a deer trail across from me, and I got out of the car, taking the cage, and walked fifty yards or so into the woods.

The raccoons were trembling, very aware something was up. I put the cage down on the carpet of needles and flipped the top open.

"Go on, boys. I guess you're boys."

Both lifted themselves from the cage and plopped to the ground. I expected them to bolt but instead they looked at me as if asking, "Are you sure? You sure about this?" And then they ran off into the trees.

I walked back to the car and sat on the hood. The crumpled pack in my shirt pocket held my last two cigarettes and I smoked both of them and watched day become night. I laughed some more and thought about how, or if, I was going to continue my search. All I had left was seven dollars and change and a half tank of gas.

Turned out it didn't matter. Two hours later, at a roadside farm, I found the bus.

And my old man.

Chapter Eleven

—

THE BUS WAS PARTIALLY HIDDEN — THOUGH NOT INTENTION-ally, I think — beside a galvanized metal grain silo. And if not for the light from the Caddie bouncing off the reflectors of about three dozen vehicles lining both sides of the road, I would have passed it by; speeding along, unaware, into the night.

As it was, I thought someone at the farm must have died and neighbors had come to call with casseroles and comfort, and I slowed a bit out of respect. And then I saw light spilling from the big, wide-open doors of what appeared to be a barn and glimpsed movement within. Then I saw the bus, covered in the shadow of the silo, and I stopped in the middle of the road, staring, before pulling into the driveway of the farmhouse.

There was a voice coming from the barn. A loud booming voice. Reverend Sam's voice. I wasn't yet close enough to decipher what he was saying, but the mesmerizing rhythm he used in his sales pitch rolled out of the barn door like a force of nature. My dislike for the man surged inside me, and I sat for a moment wondering at my approach. Maybe I'd barge in all indignant and loudly demand an explanation for my old man's kidnapping. I pictured the Reverend stammering and stuttering in

embarrassment in front of his congregation when I forced
him to reveal his plan. Or maybe I'd stay in back of the
crowd, silent, and wait for his eyes to fall on me then
watch him wilt with the knowledge he'd been caught.

I was out of the car and walking toward the barn, trying to decide what to do, when his words became clear.
And I stopped, confused.

"And now," Reverend Sam said, "y'all have all heard
enough from me so I'm gonna sit down and be quiet for
awhile! Bet y'all never thought y'all would hear that, now
did ya'?" There was laughter from the barn. "Awright,
now! Here's the man y'all really need t' listen to! Brother
Austin!"

I stepped through the doorway. I had to see.

It wasn't a barn, really, but a big chemical storage shed,
built from creosote posts and sawmill oak. The floor was
concrete, stained yellow and purple, the color of a fading
bruise, by years of spilled pesticides and manmade nutri-
ents. And when I breathed, I was half-choked by the tang
of dust and the sting of old poisons.

But those who had come to see the show, sixty or more
people, seemed not to notice and sat comfortably upon
bags of triple-15 or bales of straw. It was hot and I
watched more than one bead of sweat crawl from a hair-
line to darken the collar of a well-washed, worn work
shirt. No children cried. Ankle high, leather work boots
lay silent; there were no impatient scuffles upon the dusty
floor. There was no rustling of clothing. It was quiet. And
all eyes were on my father.

He'd appeared from nowhere, it seemed, and stood
upon the back of an empty hay wagon. The change from
not too many days before was startling. His hospital pal-
lor had absorbed some sun and the sunken eyes and

cheeks had fleshed a bit. The once carefully crafted head of hair was more shaggy now and looked good. And the Kmart clothing — prewashed jeans and a cotton shirt opened at the throat — fit him like they should.

And then he spoke. Not in the voice he'd cultivated through the years to rise above all others, but in the voice he was born with.

"This," he said, raising his arms as much as the recent surgery would allow, as if embracing everyone in the room, "is a gift. This night, this roof over our heads, that baby in your arms, sir, and the closeness of your friend beside you. The rising of the sun tomorrow. Gifts freely given but more often than not taken for granted. I did. For years I looked at all this as something owed to me. And like a child surrounded by piles of colored paper on Christmas morning, each gift I opened was tossed aside and ignored in hopes of a bigger and better gift yet to come. And then, at what seems to be the end of my life, I realized what I'd done. And I was sorry for myself." He'd been pacing slowly back and forth across the back of the wagon with all eyes upon him, but he stopped and stood silent with his head bowed. No one moved. I doubt anyone breathed. I didn't.

He raised his head and smiled a smile I'd never seen from him before. A real smile.

"But I found I had two freely given gifts left," he said. "The first of these was realizing what I'd missed, what I'd ignored. The second gift is a chance to appreciate it all now and to give you the gift of awareness in return. Maybe none of you needs to be reminded of what you've been given. I hope not. I hope all of you here wake up every morning and marvel at the air that fills your lungs. Or laugh in delight at the fact you're able to breath at all.

I hope you look at the ones you love and can love them just a little bit more. I hope for the rest of your days you can walk through this world in awe at what you've been given. I hope you can. I hope."

The last thing on this earth I'd expected to come upon was my old man telling a crowd of people he longed for the simple things in life. No . . . the last thing I expected was to hear him tell it and believe he was sincere. But I really wanted to believe he was; the other people in the room sure did. As he continued speaking, I scanned the room. Everyone was gazing at him, wrapped up in his words.

And then I saw Reverend Sam sitting on a stack of bagged feed along one wall of the shed. But he wasn't all aglow in multicolored, sequined clothing. Instead, he actually wore normal, everyday apparel. And he looked different, like a tired, old man. I guess he felt the weight of my stare because he turned and looked at me. He winked and grinned.

I knew then there was still a scam in the making — that my old man was part of the plan, somehow, and using all his skills as a politician to lead these people along. The pretty words I'd heard seemed to rustle along the concrete floor like dry, dead leaves. I just shook my head at Reverend Sam and his grin, surrendering the game.

He was still grinning at me when I jumped, startled by an all-too-familiar sharp poke in the ribs. Miss Emma stood beside me with the wooden spoon in her hand and a scowl on her face.

"Still ain't eatin' like you supposed to, I see. I guess I got to get you fed, too, along with everybody else. What took you so long? And close your mouth, boy!" She turned and shuffled out the door. "I swear! Standin' there gawpin' like some kinda damned ol' crazy man! Well come on! You better eat while you can!"

I grabbed her and gave her a hug.

"Miss Emma! Thank God there's somebody who hasn't lost their mind!" I babbled. "We can leave as soon as we can get the old man in the car. You might have to help me, though. He doesn't look like he's going to go easy."

Somehow, in my embrace, she'd drawn the spoon up and she rapped me hard on the head.

"I ain't goin' nowhere!" she yelled in a whisper. "And neither is the Senator! He's exactly where he wants to be and so am I! Now put me down, Blue, 'fore Carl sees and gets jealous!"

I dropped her and rubbed my head. "Sure you're coming with me," I said. "What do you want to stay here for? I'm here to take y'all home. I've been driving all over Georgia looking for y'all. Everything's okay now. We can leave."

Miss Emma wasn't paying any attention to me. She was looking over at the side of the barn.

"It's alright, Carl," she said into the shadows. "It's just Blue. He might act a little crazy, but he's family."

"Carl? Who's Carl?" I asked.

A very large figure stepped from around the corner and I recognized Reverend Sam's bus driver. He folded his arms across his chest. Carl took up a lot of space.

Miss Emma sighed and giggled and then floated over to Carl. She placed a tiny hand on one of his basketball-sized biceps and patted her hair.

"Carl's my honey now," she giggled and then batted her eyelashes like some silent movie queen. "Ain't you Carl?"

Though I didn't see him twitch nor hear a sound from the vast mass of man, Carl must have responded to suit

Miss Emma, because she sighed again.

"Oh, Carl," she said. "Ain't no need in you bein' jealous a' Blue. I've found my man!" She stroked his arm.

"Goddammit, Miss Emma, what's going on here?" Carl or no Carl, I had to speak before I exploded. "Will you please explain to me what all this is about?" My plea for information bounced off their backs and fell to the farm yard, though, because they had turned and walked into the darkness between the silo and bus, Miss Emma cooing and giggling at Carl as they went. I had no choice but to follow.

What I found at the front of the bus, on the other side of the silo, was a refugee camp of sorts. In a loose circle, about thirty paces across, tents of blue tarps and bed sheets were strung up with baling wire. Mismatched tables and lawn chairs were scattered around inside the circle. Camp lanterns, hung by nails on several hastily placed poles, cast yellow light and lured moths and brown beetles from all corners of the county. In the middle was a big fire of pine, ringed with stones and burning hot and smokey. Atop the stones was a metal grill. Beside the fire were two Coleman propane stoves set up on aluminum camp stands. The stoves were crowded with big, metal pots and the grill was layered with fryer halves, dripping and spitting into the fire.

And tending it all was a lady of twenty-five years or so, dressed in jeans and an oversized man's shirt tied up at the waist. Her face was tanned brown, like an old leather belt, and she kept pushing strands of auburn hair from her sweaty face with one hand while stirring and poking the food with the other. But she was beaming as she worked, her white teeth damn near outshining the lanterns. A small army of kids, from the ages of six to thirteen or fourteen, made steady treks back and forth from the fire to the rear door of the farmhouse, retrieving utensils and bowls and such at direction from the lady in command.

The odor of blue smoke, combined with the sound of sizzling and the flicker of the flame, drew serious saliva and I think I stood there drooling for a moment, hypnotized. The sleeping, primal part of my brain concerned with the magic of fire and the need to crack bones with my teeth and suck marrow stirred awake.

"Damn, Blue! Wipe your mouth! You embarrassin' me!" Miss Emma poked me with a bony finger. "Go on an' get somethin' to eat 'fore the rest of 'em get out here." She muttered something to Carl about my manners and pushed me toward the fire.

I stumbled into the circle of light and the lady cooking graced me with that beautiful smile.

"Well, hey," she said. "Welcome to my place. Welcome. Y'all lettin' out in there? You ready to eat?" She turned and spoke to one of the children, a girl, who sped over to a table and grabbed a chipped china plate patterned with blue flowers.

"Thank you, darlin'," she said, taking the plate from the girl and heaping it with beans and corn from the pots and spearing a half of a chicken off the grill. She handed me the plate and looked over my shoulder.

"Where're the rest?" she asked. She spied Miss Emma, who was entering the bus with Carl, and called out to her. "Miss Emma, they about through in there?"

"Naw, hon. It'll be awhile, yet," she answered. "You jus' go on and feed that boy there and then put him to work. If he gives you any trouble, just smack his jaws. That's all he understands." She disappeared into the bus and the doors shushed closed.

The woman looked at me and laughed. And I found myself snatched into stupidity by eyes so big and so startlingly green I couldn't speak. "That gonna be enough for ya'?" she asked.

"Uh," I replied. I barely even felt the hot beans spilling from my tilted plate and scalding my hand.

She laughed again. "Well, if it's not, you just let me know. There's plenty here." And then she squinted at me through the smoke and her lips formed an "o" of surprise. She grabbed my arm and dragged me to one of the lanterns and stood studying my face. "You look just like . . . somebody." She gasped. "Brother Austin! You look just like Brother Austin! You could be his son or somethin'! Are you?"

The eyes plucked my brain from its static state and though the urge to deny relationship was strong, I wanted to say whatever it took to keep this lady from going away.

"My name's Blue," I told her. "Blue Belew. And, yeah, the man you call Brother Austin is my dad. I'm here to take him home."

"What? Take him home? You can't do that . . . only the Lord can, and only when He's ready." She glanced at the fire and pushed me toward a table. "You go on over there and sit down," she commanded. "I'll be back in a minute." And she darted over to the stoves.

I sat down at a rickety, old cafeteria table and tried to eat. But the way she moved as she led the children through their work and tended the food distracted me and barely a morsel found its way to my mouth. She nodded at my plate as she slid into a chair across the table from me.

"Not hungry?" she asked and then grinned. "You don't

want me get Miss Emma out here to feed you, now do ya'? She acts like she's got your number."

I went stupid again at the way she placed her forearms on the table and leaned toward me. There was a thin sheen of perspiration on her lip and it, along with those emerald eyes, sparkled with light captured from the lanterns.

She looked alarmed. "Blue? Are you okay?"

"Uh . . . yeah. Yeah. I was just wondering . . . wondering what your name is." My face went hot with embarrassment when I heard my voice. The words I'd spoken sounded to me like the gruntings of some great, retarded beast. I was appalled.

"Oh! I'm sorry." She'd somehow deciphered the incomprehensible mutterings spilling from my mouth and thrust her hand out. "I'm Josephine. Josephine Lee. Everybody calls me Jo, though. I wish you would, too."

"Jo," I whispered, taking her hand in mine. And though it was callused and scarred, it was a beautiful hand and I felt oafish enough to crush it just by breathing too hard. I held her hand just a beat too long, and when I realized this I dropped it like I'd been burnt.

"Oh, gosh!" she yelped and leaped from the chair. "I'll be back. You stay put." She ran to the backdoor of the house to help one of the children descending the steps with a tottering stack of china.

I pushed my plate away and laid my head on the table, cradled in my arms.

"What an idiot," I muttered to myself. "That's just great, you fuckin' idiot. Why didn't you just reach out and start groping her?" I tried to liquify and soak into the table top. When she came back — if she came back — all she'd see would be a puddle of slime she could wipe away with a handful of paper towels.

"God, you have to watch 'em every minute," I heard her say as she sat in the chair beside me.

I could feel her. She was eighteen inches away but I could feel her.

"I'm sorry," I said, my words muffled by my arms

"What?" she asked. "Are you sick or somethin', Blue?"

I lifted my head and dared to look at her. "I'm sorry for scaring you off," I told her.

She looked confused for a moment, then she laughed. "You didn't scared me off," she said, batting my shoulder with one of those perfect hands. "Those young'uns just keep me runnin' all the time."

"Are they all yours?" I asked. "The kids?"

She laughed again. "Well, yeah, I guess you could say they're all mine. Or I'm all theirs. I'm all they have." She grew quiet and her smile went away. "They're my brothers and sisters."

The unexplainable relief I felt — as if I lacked gravity and was floating an inch or two above the chair seat — at discovering the children weren't hers was short-lived when I realized I was responsible for her mood.

"I'm sorry," I said again. "I didn't mean to ask questions I shouldn't be asking."

Her smile reappeared. "Do you always go around apologizin'? I mean, how are you gonna know if you don't ask?" She looked out at the children, who were running around inside the circle, playing some just-invented game. "They are mine, though. Them and the farm. Mama and Daddy both died a while back, just one year apart, and left those babies with me." She'd drifted off and was staring so deep into the distance that I began to worry she had somehow gone away. I left her alone, though, waiting for her to come back. And while I waited, I looked at her. And looked.

Jo breathed deep and shook her head, awakening. "You're lucky, Blue, to have your Daddy around."

I snorted, an altogether horrible sound.

"What's that supposed to mean?" Jo asked.

"I guess you don't know my dad too well, do you? Or haven't known him long enough." She seemed to want more. "Look," I said, "I heard the line he and the midget have been throwing around and, believe me, it's just that, a line of bullshit. They'll suck those people dry in there, in that barn, and then go on to the next place and do the same thing. Looks to me like they've already taken you for a ride." I flapped my hand at the fire and the food.

Jo leaned away from me and narrowed her eyes. I felt bad for telling her the truth, but I wanted her to know. She started to speak, then stopped, shaking her head.

"No," she said after a moment, "I'm not going to let anybody take what I've got away from me."

Relief. I'd saved someone.

But Jo continued. "Not even you," she said, "his own son, can take away what he gave me today. It's the message that counts, not how it got here. And I don't think . . . no, I know your daddy and Reverend Sam aren't the way you're tryin' to tell me they are." She pushed away from the table and started to stand. "I've got work to do. And, by the way, they brought all this food with 'em. Enjoy."

I don't know why, but the last thing in the world I wanted was for her to go away not liking me. I grabbed her arm.

"Please, Jo," I said, "I need to know what's happening here." She didn't try to pull away so I kept talking. "I don't know if it's really so, but the man in the barn seems to be a lot different from the one I thought I always knew. Let me tell you a story. Please."

Whether it was from pity or from a real interest in what I had to say, I don't know, but she sat and almost knocked me flat again with those big, green eyes.

"Go ahead," she said.

Once again I told my story. And for the first time I listened to what I was telling. It was as if I were sitting on the other side of the table watching my own mouth move. And when I got to the part about finally catching up with the bus and seeing my old man talk his talk from the back of that wagon, a light, a dim one, but a light, must have appeared in my eyes.

"See what I mean," Jo said, smiling. Finally. Smiling at me again. "Until that bus there pulled up into the yard this mornin', and Reverend Sam got off to ask if they could camp here and use the barn for a meetin', I was the most pitiful person in this part of Georgia. Had been for a year. I had all these kids to take care of. And this farm. And all I could see, no matter how far in the future I looked, was me wakin' up every mornin' doin' the same things. Over and over again." She took my hand. "And then your daddy, Blue, your daddy seemed to know this and he took me aside and smiled at me and told me how good he thought it must be to have what I have. It wasn't the words, though, Blue, but the way he said them. And the more he talked the more I believed he meant what he said: 'How good it must be'." She turned her smile from me to the children, and then to the sky and the bugs and the way the blue smoke was being batted about by the breeze. "We talked for a long time, Blue. And you know, he's made a big impression on me. I kinda like it." She was still smiling out at the night and at the things, the bits and pieces, that made up her world. All was well with her.

It wouldn't have taken much for me to sit there watching her for the rest of the night. And I wanted to tell her so, but that moment was broken by a discreet cough. We both jumped as if bitten.

Standing behind us, grinning and giggling, was a group of older people being entertained by my display of mooning. Some carried canes and some were propped up on walkers. Others were supported by the people beside them. All were thin and looked tired almost to the point of collapse. And though their eyes were sunk deep and ringed dark from fatigue or from the effects of ever-present physical pain, I could sense a light of being alive in each one of them that I had not seen two weeks earlier. Before, they'd been pitiful, a herd of husks, bags of flesh waiting for, expecting, that last bit of animation to vanish from their bodies. But now, though physically the same, more than a spark of spirit surrounded them. I could almost feel a fire. One old man winked an eye and raised a slow, palsied thumbs-up in my direction.

Time to wonder was out of the question because Jo dragged me from my chair and pulled me with her.

"Come on, Blue. Help me get these folks situated." She turned and placed two fingers in her mouth, whistling at the kids, who immediately quit their playing and ran to her.

"Let's help these people to their tents, y'all, and get 'em fed," she told them. The children, six of them, darted eagerly over to the cluster of old men and women and took an elbow or a hand in each of their own and began to guide them toward the tents.

I heard the old ones commenting on the manners displayed every time one of the children said "yes, ma'am" or "no, sir." Or how pretty the little girls were and how handsome the boys were. A lady with a familiar green scarf covering her bald head looked at me as she passed.

"How are you, ma'am?" I asked.

"Oh, I'm fine. I'm fine," she said, and stroked the hair of the eight-year-old girl helping her along. "How could I not be on such a pretty night?" She smiled at me and I saw the beginning of tears in her eyes.

A tall, skinny black man with an aluminum cane was shuffling in my direction, and I stepped up and offered my hand. I remembered him from my first night on the road, coming home.

"Can I help you, sir? It's Curtis, right?"

"Naw, naw," he said, shaking his head. "I believe I can make it awright. This ol' stick here is all I'm needin'." He stopped and looked into my face. "How you know my name?" he asked. "I don't like it when people I don't know know me. You ain't with the gummint, are you?"

I laughed. "No, sir, I'm not with the government. You might not remember, but I saw you one night at a restaurant beside the interstate a while back. Can I get you some food, maybe?"

"Lord God, yes, son!" he said. "I won't be able t' eat it, but I still sure do enjoy lookin' at a mess a' meat an' beans."

I walked beside him to his tent and helped him as he situated himself under the blue and white checked sheet. A pile of pillows propped him up and his legs were blanketed with a multicolored quilt. He seemed comfortable enough but I was a little angry that this sick old man had only the ground to rest on.

"I can't believe this," I said to him. "You'd think they'd at least find a cheap motel."

"Cain't believe what, son? Brother Austin and the Reverend didn't have nothin' to do with us campin' out. This is what we wanted to do." Curtis scooted back against the pillows and smoothed the quilt. "Hell, I've slept better the past few nights than I have since this goddam cancer got me. I growed up with cracks in the wall a' my house big enough t' throw a cat through. This night air's the best thang in the world for a sick man. An' las' night . . . las' night I had m'own cricket. It's hard to believe music that sweet was comin' outta a bug's ass." He closed his eyes and rested his head. "Now go on, son, and get me that plate. An' put two pieces a' chicken on it." He was asleep before I could back out of the tent.

Jo was kneeling beside one of the women in another tent, holding a syringe in one hand. She was patting the woman's arm.

"What's that?" I asked her.

"Antibiotics. She's got a cold," she told me. "That's a lot worse than it sounds, too. When cancer reaches this stage, any little thing is intensified. Her immune system isn't quite what it used to be." The lady grimaced when Jo administered the shot but smiled up at her when she finished.

"Thank you, hon. You've got an easy touch. Thank you."

"Yes, ma'am," said Jo, "but wouldn't you rather be in the house? You wouldn't be puttin' a soul out. There's plenty of room."

"Lord, no, girl. As close as I am to leavin' it don't matter where I lay," she said. "Besides, if I'm gonna be spendin' eternity in the ground I need to practice a little by sleepin' on it." She cackled at the expressions on our faces. "Y'all go on, now, and help the rest of them old geezers out there. I need to sleep."

We went from tent to tent, Jo and I did, tending to those who were ready for bed and feeding those who weren't. Some needed medication — antibiotics or pain killers — and Jo dispensed it all with an ease and an empathy that amazed me. She joked and chided most of the time but damn near commanded when she had to.

"You act like you've done this before," I said after I'd watched her give her third or fourth injection.

"Well, Mama and Daddy were sick for a long time," she told me as we walked to the fire for more food. "They both had cancer and I was the only one old enough to take care of 'em. It's not so hard. You just gotta remember that the person layin' there on that bed means somethin' to somebody . . . that maybe they spent a lot of years of their life cleanin' up after and takin' care of a child of their own." She handed me a plate and looked over my shoulder. "You know, even you weren't born able to take care of yourself. Whether you remember or not, there was somebody there for you." And she nodded toward the bus.

I turned and saw some of the people who'd come to hear the preaching. Apparently the sermon was over. Standing in the middle of a cluster of the faithful, almost a head taller than those around him, was my old man basking in their admiration like he was Elvis. As if by design, the crowd parted and I could see Reverend Sam standing beside him, shaking hands and slapping backs. Together, they turned to look at me, then excused themselves and strode across the camp, smiling toward me and Jo.

Chapter Twelve
—

THINGS BEGAN TO HAPPEN PRETTY FAST. JO WAS STANDING beside me beaming at my old man and Reverend Sam as they came our way. I wanted to leave, to go away, but somehow she divined my need to flee and took hold of my arm as if I belonged to her. Her touch paralyzed me and I stood rigid in that one spot as if I'd sprouted there.

Until that moment I never knew what it meant to be frozen by emotion. On my right, clutching my arm, was a woman I'd met only two hours before who had touched me more than anyone I'd known in my life. The feel of her fingers burnt me and sent streamers of electricity to my chest, affecting my breathing and the flow of blood to my brain.

I didn't think about love. Not then. I was focused on the smiling man in front of me. A man I'd known all my life but who was a stranger to me. His ice-blue eyes were all I could see and I searched them with my own, trying to find anything that would give me a hint as to what was happening with him. And I was scared. Confrontations with my old man always had only one outcome: him winning, me losing.

They stopped a couple of feet from us and I held out my hand, wanting to at least be civil. But my old man ignored it and almost leaped forward, grabbing me in a bear hug and lifting me a few inches off the ground. He dropped me probably from the pain in his chest, and I stumbled, feeling myself burn bright red with embarrassment. Reverend Sam laughed and Jo covered her mouth with her hand, hiding a smile.

My father took my shoulders, helping me steady myself and himself. We stood face to face. And I continued my search for clues. I was startled to see those ice-blue eyes had thawed, had taken on a warmer glow. There was a look of contentment in his eyes now as if he had just completed a job and done it well. I stepped away from him.

"It's good to see you, son." I couldn't remember the last time he'd called me that. "I'll have to admit, though, I was a little worried for awhile. Didn't know if you'd have time to catch up."

"I told ya'! I told ya' this boy was gonna find us!" Reverend Sam had sidled over to Jo and was now hopping about and grinning like some overgrown toad. "He ain't near as stupid as he looks, now is he, darlin'?" Jo had taken Sam's hand and was giving him the smile I thought of as my own.

It was hard to breathe and I could barely see anymore. Loathing for Sam, jealous that Jo would grace him with a touch, and bewilderment at the visible change in my old man all blended together and blanketed me. I couldn't speak.

"Aw, Sam," my dad said, chuckling. "Leave him alone, now. He's tired, I suspect, and things are probably a bit overwhelming. Am I right, Blue?" He asked me with a look of kindness that seemed utterly alien upon his face. "You go on and rest up a bit while me and Sam check on everybody . . . even though I'm sure Jo's ministrations leave nothing to be desired." He turned to her, smiled, and gave her a slight bow, begging her forgiveness. She beamed back, increasing the tightness of my chest in the process.

"We've a lot to talk about, Blue," he said over his shoulder as he and Reverend Sam walked away toward the tents. "There are some things I need for you to hear."

"God! Aren't they great?"

Jo's voice helped peel the blanket from my body but it was a few moments before I was able to speak.

"Blue? Wasn't it good to see him?" she asked me.

"I . . . I don't know," I said. "I really . . . really don't know." I sucked in a great lung full of night air and held it a bit before letting it go. "My old man . . . Sam . . . oh, hell, Jo. I don't know."

"Come on," she said and guided me to the fire then pushed me down into a chair. "You go on and do what your daddy says and rest. And, Blue, why don't you just try and let things happen the way they're gonna happen, okay? You can't keep forcin' people to fit; sometimes they outgrow those holes you've dug for 'em." And she kissed me on the cheek then disappeared into the house.

I sat staring into the fire. What Jo had said unnerved me more than the kiss had. Two different people from two different places — not connected in any way that I knew of — had spoken almost identical words to me. Had told me I was too quick to keep people pegged, wouldn't allow them room to move. I wondered if I was that easy to read, if I was really that hard on people. The fire sucked me in and I sat for a long, long time, mesmerized and hypnotized and confounded by the picture I was presenting myself. The self-analysis by firelight didn't do much for my mood so I pulled out of it, shuddering alert.

Miss Emma was walking across the circle toward me

with Carl gliding a step behind her like the shadow of a train. She had that Miss Emma look on her face and I knew I was in for a major battle.

"Blue," she said, standing in front of me with one hand on her hip and the other in her apron pocket, fondling the spoon, "me and Carl are done here. We got to get on down the road. It's your turn to take care of your daddy now. Give me your car keys." And she thrust her hand out, palm up.

What I'd expected from her, I don't know. But it definitely wasn't this. I gaped at her. Then I laughed. And laughed again. I was still laughing when Carl stepped out from behind her and bent down and glowered into my face. He was not smiling. My laughter died. Miss Emma patted his shoulder.

"You back on up now, Carl, baby. We don't need none a' that . . . yet." She glanced at me and bumped Carl out of the way with her hip. "I mean it," she said. "I want them car keys. You won't be needin' 'em no more."

It wasn't funny anymore. Too much had happened in too little time and I was tired. I felt as though I'd stepped into some alternate universe where absolutely nothing was what it appeared to be. And now all I wanted to do was find my way back to the world I'd come from. I stood up to leave.

"I don't know what's happening here, Miss Emma, but I've just decided I don't want any part in it," I declared. "You can't have the car; it's not mine. And I'm not hanging around to take responsibility for the old man, that's not mine either." Carl tensed up at the tone of my voice but Miss Emma soothed him with a cluck of her tongue. "Your new boyfriend can try to strong-arm me if he wants to; I don't care anymore. Whatever it is all of y'all are into now is fine with me. It's fine. But I'm out of it, Miss Emma. If you have a message for Mama or the rest of the family, I'll be glad to pass it on. I'll even tell 'em y'all are all okay, that they don't have a thing to worry about, despite the fact I think you and the old man and definitely Reverend Sam have all gone as crazy as hell." I rubbed my hand over my face then took a great gulp of air and let it out.

"Now, if you don't mind, I'm going to find Jo and tell her goodbye. She's about the best thing I've come across this entire trip." The words pulled a little pain out with them. I didn't really want to tell her goodbye.

Miss Emma stood smiling as if she hadn't heard a word I'd said. She shook her head and chuckled. Others behind me joined her and I turned to see my dad and Reverend Sam laughing like they'd just heard the greatest joke in the world.

The Reverend stopped laughing long enough to wink at me.

"You ain't goin' nowhere, boy," he said. "You heard your daddy say he's got some things you need to hear. Show him some respect and give him the time he's askin' for."

I spun around, looking from face to face to face. They were all laughing at me for no reason I could figure other than that I was laughable to them. But, amazingly, their laughing didn't make me mad.

"I'm gone," I said, shaking my head. "I'm gone." And I walked from the circle of tents, past the silo and out to my car. The others had left and I sat alone, deflated, in the Caddie wanting badly to turn the key and leave but unable to make my hands move.

Sitting by myself, away from other human beings,

seemed to be what I needed. Bats and bugs fluttered about above, fleeing or feeding, and it calmed me. The darkness seeped into my body and patted and smoothed everything back in line. My brow relaxed and my brain took a deep breath.

Many miles ago I'd given up trying to interpret the trip; things seemed to happen as they would. But I must admit I had never foreseen my running away from the outcome. Hell, I didn't even know what I was looking for anymore. I'd found the old man but my fantasies of being his salvation didn't fit. He was the same self-assured, in-control person he'd always been. Only . . . different. A difference I'd questioned, had suspected, but one he seemed to wear well. And the really odd thing was he'd said there was something he needed for me to hear. He needed me. A true, honest-to-God, out-of-left-field, never-expected statement spilling from his lips. And I wanted to believe he needed me but . . . but the setting wasn't right.

I was bothered by something. His strength pissed me off.

The heat of the South Georgia night didn't account for the rise in temperature in my face. It was embarrassment. And it was shame. And I thought back to the beginning of my trip, to the call from Amy. When I hung up the phone, as I was packing my bag, I'd felt a twinge of glee at the old man's condition. I'd pictured breezing into Dura, then striding into the hospital prepared to take care of things while my dad, all pale and drawn, lay moaning away in his bed. I'd pictured standing over him, patting his hand, and murmuring that everything was going to be alright.

But instead I'd found him as strong as ever and for some reason it made me mad.

The screen door of the farmhouse squealed open and Jo

stood on the front steps illuminated by the porch light. She exchanged a few words with Miss Emma and headed my way. I panicked as she approached, not wanting her to see me painted into the corner of my revelation. But the sight of her made me motionless and she opened the car door and slid in beside me; her leg touched mine.

She just sat there. I didn't speak; afraid I would bleat or babble and she would jump out and run screaming into the night. After a while she sighed and brushed a strand of that auburn hair from her face and turned to me.

"I guess you were just gonna leave without sayin' a word, huh?"

"Yeah," I said, a little amazed at my honesty. "I think it's time I got out of here. I've got a long way to go."

"Wow," she said, "I've never had that effect on anybody that I know of." She smiled. "Too fast for ya', huh?"

The babbling began.

"Oh, no! It's not you, Jo! I'd love to stay here with you and . . . " She arched an eyebrow and my face grew hot.

"And what?"

"That's . . . that's not what I mean," I stammered. "What I mean is . . . what I mean is, I would like to know you better. But . . . but all this . . . all these things happening kind of get in the way."

"Well, then take care of these things, Blue. If all this," she waved a hand toward the bus and the flicker of the fire behind the silo, "if all this is what's in the way, then move it. And I don't mean walk around or away from it, either. Put your hands on it. Get in the middle of it and find out what it's gonna take, Blue, for you to get to where you're goin'. Where you're goin' in here." And she reached out and touched my forehead and then the middle of my chest.

"And when you find out," she said, "you come back here and tell me all about it. Okay? Promise?"

I nodded and before I could speak, she kissed my lips and reached across me, opening the door and pushing me out.

"Go on and talk to your daddy," she commanded. "I got babies to put to bed." And then she was gone.

The hundred-yard walk back to camp seemed miles long and paved with snarls of barbed wire that kept snagging my legs and holding me back.

But eventually I made it and found the old man, Reverend Sam, and Miss Emma sitting in front of the bus in scavenged, aluminum lawn chairs, laughing and drinking bourbon straight from the bottle. Carl stood behind Miss Emma with his arms folded like some great, stone sentry. They stopped partying when they spotted me and fell silent. My dad seemed genuinely glad to see me but the good Reverend looked all smug and superior, as if he'd foretold my return.

The strength to speak came from not looking at my father. I avoided his gaze as if it would sting me or he would somehow ferret out my conclusions in the car from the way my eyes moved. My target was Reverend Sam.

"First of all," I said, striding up and pointing at him, "I don't like you. You're an asshole and a miserable, little bastard." I directed my finger at the tents behind us. "What you've done to these people is . . . is beyond belief. How in the hell you can consider yourself a human being is something I'll never figure out. And why anybody . . . anybody would decide to follow you anywhere, play along with your little game, is another mystery. You should be in jail for what you've done."

My tirade was going so well I'd lost focus on his face. I

paused to breathe and heard nothing but silence. And I looked at Reverend Sam and saw him slumped in the chair. His grin was gone and he sat engulfed in his clothes like a doll dressed in grown-up garments. The once vibrant, red hair — his or not — was now wispy and brittle and his skin was gray with sickness. He was pitiful and I was embarrassed for him, and myself, but I couldn't stop. I couldn't stop.

"You're a nasty, little fucker, Sam," I ranted, wishing I could somehow disappear into the ground and at the same time hoping the filth I spat at him would direct attention away from me. "The best thing you could do for anybody would be to slit your own . . ."

"Blue!"

My head was snatched around as if I'd been slapped, and my eyes locked with my father's. His old eyes were back and I felt a bloom of frost run up my spine. My breathing stopped dead in mid-draw. But I saw an instant of uncertainty spark in his eyes and for the first time in my life, I felt my own turn into orbs of ice. We stared at each other for a long, long time, a stand-off disturbed only by the sounds of Reverend Sam sobbing. And then my father reached over and put his hand on Sam's shoulder. The old man had blinked. He blinked!

A giggle of victory began to bubble up from somewhere inside me but it never passed my lips. The Blue I'd always tried to be wouldn't let it happen. Somehow he'd found a way to crawl from the corner he'd been cowering in and put a stop to that last bit of nastiness.

I was trembling, near collapse, when someone put a hand on my back.

"Sit down, child," Miss Emma said, and I leaned on her like an invalid as she led me to a chair. Carl appeared as if from nowhere and placed a plastic cup half full of bourbon in my hands.

And I sat and watched my dad console Sam, murmuring and reassuring, as the little man cried.

"That boy's right, Austin," I heard him say over and over again. "He's right. The thangs I done in my life shouldn't never be done by nobody. That boy's speakin' the truth."

I couldn't hear the words my old man spoke but, after what seemed hours, Sam sat up straight and rubbed his eyes with his tiny fists then laughed softly.

"I know, Austin. And I thank ya'. I thank ya'."

My dad made himself comfortable in his chair and turned his attention to me. The frozen-stone eyes were gone. He uncapped the bourbon and jiggled it in my direction. I declined.

"You know, Blue," he said, pausing to pull a swallow from the bottle, "everybody here . . . everybody . . . has done things they're not proud of, things that leave them on the fringes, on the outside, of the rest of the world. Some stay there, are never reclaimed by their brothers and sisters. Others dart in and out getting dirty for awhile, then come back to cleanse themselves. And then . . . then there are the ones like me . . . and like Sam, here . . . who need something to tap them on the shoulder and smack them full in the face before they're able to pull themselves back in amongst humankind. Like dying. Yeah, dying'll do it for you, won't it, Sam?" He turned and smiled at the man beside him.

"You got that right, Austin," he said, smiling back.

"The point is, Blue," the old man continued, "is it all comes down to how you deal with it when you finally come back that counts. And, for me, realizing and believing in and appreciating all the things I've turned my back on for so many years is my way, my small way, of making amends. That's all. And if my message helps anybody, anybody at all, well . . . it's a good thing, isn't it?"

An uneasiness had settled over me as I sat listening to one of the strongest people I'd ever known strip himself bare. They all seemed to be waiting for me to speak and I squirmed a bit.

"Yeah, well, I guess if they have to hear it from somebody, it may as well be from someone who's so filled with the Holy Spirit." My reply was meant to be snotty and sarcastic — filled with venom and fine-honed to a razor edge, but I was spent and the words tumbled out and lay flat on the ground.

"I don't know if it's holy, son," my dad said, looking off into the night, "but I know it's here. And out there and beneath our feet. We walk through it every day, breathing it in and having it lay upon our faces. If we let it in, it's in our voices and in the way we look at people and in how we act. Some might call it holy; it fits. All I know is that it's here if we want it."

Amazingly, Sam laughed. He'd reanimated and was once again grinning his big-toothed grin.

"Your daddy missed his callin', boy," he chortled, slapping his knee. "He shoulda' been a preacher instead of a politician. Damn, Austin, you sure as hell got a tongue on ya.'"

"They're one in the same, Sam," my dad said. "There's a lot of talking from both of 'em. I've finally figured out, though, none of it means a thing unless you're telling people what they already know. Politicians and preachers both tend to treat folks as if they don't have brains. People know what's right. But it's good to have somebody reaffirm what you believe every once in a while."

"What's this got to do with me?" I blurted out. "I can hear all the Sunday school stuff I want just by turning on the radio." I swallowed and my throat clicked dry. What I was going to say didn't come easy. "Dad, I . . . I'm glad to see you've found something to believe in. I really am. And I'm . . . sorry for doubting your sincerity. And I apologize to you, Reverend Sam, for the way I talked to you. No . . . for the way I cussed you like a dog. But I don't think any of this has a thing to do with me and I'd like to leave now. There's nothing I can do for y'all."

The old man was nodding as if he'd expected to hear everything I'd said and was in agreement. Sam was smiling a normal person's smile at me and he murmured "That's awright, boy."

We all sat silent for awhile. The bottle made three passes, then another was opened. Periodically, the lull was broken by slaps at mosquitoes or the pop of the fire. Twice, Carl lumbered off only to return to feed the flames with big chunks of pine that threw up showers of sparks when they were laid within the ring of stones. The burning bits swirled and floated and danced up toward the sky, then would wink out like tiny, short-lived cousins of the stars. And then the show would be over and everyone would sigh as if having wished they could have ridden up on one of those flickers of light.

The bottle passed to me again but I waved it away. I had to leave.

"Will you stay, Blue?"

How my dad figured I was preparing my departure I don't know, but I relaxed back in my seat and inclined my head toward him. He continued speaking.

"I don't expect you to all of a sudden look upon me as

a wonderful person, Blue. Hell, too much time's gotten in the way for that to happen. And you've seen me walking through this world throwing that time away. I know that . . . I know. And I know you might be wondering why I couldn't have made the change back home, with your Mama and Junior and Amy there to be part of it. Hell, Blue, I'm as confused about what's going on with me as the rest of you, and the truth is, I don't know why. But I know I like it. And another thing I know, have always known, is that if anybody would understand . . . it would be you." He'd said all this looking down at the ground or into the fire, anywhere but at me, but then he lifted his eyes to mine.

"I only have a few days left," he said. "And I want you there with me. I want somebody who knows me to be there."

A protest formed at the back of my throat. A protest to challenge what he'd said about having only days left to live. But as I looked across the fire at him, before I could blurt the words, I really saw my dad. He was sick and the look of those who rode the bus was upon him. The skin on his face was stretched tight, seemingly drawing his bones closer to the surface and creating a mask of shadows. And those eyes . . . those eyes that had so frightened me for most of my life, were sunken now and held traces of pain. The more I looked at him, the less familiar he became. It was as if my father's spirit had somehow invaded a dying man's body.

The most disturbing part of his appearance was how I must have missed it when I first saw him earlier in the evening. The vision I'd created of him — some great shambling monster, I suppose — as I rode the roads in my search had somehow obscured my view and allowed me to see only what I'd expected to see. And what I'd expected to see was not at all what sat in front of me now.

This man was almost sick to death, maybe a little bit scared, asking me to take my place beside him, my rightful place, and ride his last ride with him. And looking back, I think I also saw, in one dreadful moment of clarity, how the ride would end. How it had to end for all of them.

"I'll come," I said. "I'll come with you."

Chapter Thirteen

—

Morning flared full force in my face only a few hours after we'd celebrated, hard, my agreement to travel with Reverend Sam's revival. I woke on the ground with a cat curled up and purring on my chest and rays from the new sun piercing my eyelids and drilling through my brain to the back of my skull. A clod of dirt whizzed past my head and the cat leaped up with a hiss and sped off toward the house. I heard giggling and inched my eyeballs to the right to see Jo's brothers and sisters preparing to pepper me with a carefully selected collection of debris.

I moaned and braced myself for the punishment I probably deserved. Besides, I had no defense short of moving and I didn't yet have control of my body.

"Y'all stop that! Go on, now!" The kids scattered, laughing, and I saw Jo approaching with a mug in her hand. She stood over me with her fist on her hip and glared down at me. I tried to smile.

"I oughta pour this coffee on your head. It'd do just as much good as you drinkin' it, I imagine." She grabbed my arm and jerked me to a sitting position. "Get up!" she commanded.

I whimpered.

"Oh, shut up," she said and thrust the mug into my

hands. And then she fed me two aspirin. Her fingertips felt like moth wings fluttering against my lips.

"You probably need these," she said. I nodded. "I don't know what was goin' on, but around four o'clock this mornin' I peeped out the window and saw you and Miss Emma dancin' while Carl beat on one of the chairs with that big ol' wooden spoon of hers. Your daddy and the Reverend were clappin' and stompin' their feet." She tsked and shook her head, beginning to smile.

"Oh, yeah," I said after scalding my mouth with a sip of coffee and washing the scum away. "We kind of had a party last night. Miss Emma accused me of having no rhythm and I had to prove her wrong."

She laughed and the sound of it did more for me than the caffeine ever could. "She's right, you know. You don't have any rhythm."

"'Bout time you got up, boy!" Our moment was broken when Reverend Sam bounded up, cawwing. "Hell, we thought we was gonna hafta tie you to the top a' the bus and carry you 'round like road kill if you didn't move soon!" He made a few jerky movements I interpreted as dancing, then pointed at me and laughed like hell before strutting off.

I smiled weakly at Jo. "I guess I was a hit, huh?"

There was no response. She just looked at me.

"What?" I asked.

She sat on the ground beside me. "Last night you promised me you'd come back. Did you mean it?" She picked a blade of grass and studied it like all the answers in the world were somehow hidden in that little strip of green.

Every reason I could have ever used to somehow qualify what I'd told her the night before flashed through my mind. But I didn't need one. What I needed was the words to tell her what she did to me. I needed words that would make her understand it was hard for me to breathe for fear she would disappear when she was near me. I wanted words to describe the way my eyes tracked her wherever she went.

"Yeah," I said, as eloquent as ever, "I meant it."

And she jumped up, pulling me with her, and put her arms around me. I returned her hug, tentatively, afraid I would crush her.

"Well, get goin', then," she said, stepping away and smiling at me. "The sooner you leave, the sooner you'll be back."

I couldn't let her go.

"I will be back," I said. "You count on it."

"Oh, I'll do more than that," she laughed. "I'll come find your ass. Count on that!"

We kissed then, of course. And it was wonderful, until right about the time we were pelted by the sticks and clods of dirt that had been meant for me a few minutes earlier. Jo's siblings stood pointing and hooting at us while I grinned like an idiot.

We spent the next hour or so breaking camp and loading the bus. Reverend Sam and Miss Emma directed the operation like competing generals. Carl and my dad and me lifted and loaded and did most of the sweating. The old man stopped and sat several times, catching his breath. I could tell he didn't want us to notice, so we pretended not to. Jo administered last-minute medicines and helped the old ones onto the bus.

Then it was time to go.

I could go into how hard it was for me to see Jo standing in the front yard waving goodbye as I backed the

Caddie out and fell in behind the bus. But I barely had time to reflect. Miss Emma insisted that she ride in the Caddie with me so she could tell Carl, later, how to drive it. The five thousand times I told her there was no way she was ever going to get her hands on the car just bounced off her old head, so after awhile I quit mentioning it, hoping she'd forget.

After we gassed up, we fell into a kind of rhythm. I followed the bus, not at all concerned with where we were headed. We were going only fifty, but the first few miles of the trip Miss Emma clutched the dashboard with one hand and her arm rest with the other as if we were barreling, with no brakes, down a mountain. She calmed and alternated between telling me stories and complaining about my driving technique. I had to stop once to catch my breath from laughing at her trying to roll a cigarette for the fifth time as the wind snatched papers from her fingers and showered her with shreds of tobacco.

We stopped at noon for food and more fuel. I boarded the bus to pass out packages and was surprised to see the passengers all awake and alert, anxious for movement. I helped with medications and we hit the road again.

I opened a fresh pack of Camels, bought with money bummed from my old man, and slipped my shades on. Miss Emma snatched them off my face and placed them on her own. She looked better in them than I did, so I didn't protest.

At four o'clock we stopped at a roadside park, much like the one I'd slept in a few nights before, and the old man got off the bus holding a map and approached the car.

"This is the place," he said.

"The place for what?" I asked, looking at the concrete

picnic tables and the gravel on the ground.

"We'll stay here tonight," he told me. "People know we're comin'. They'll be here. Let's get set up."

I asked for no more explanation, and none was offered, so we unloaded the bus and set up the tents. The passengers got off and wandered about the tiny park. Some found shade beneath the trees and sat content, gazing out upon the world. Others walked around picking up pine cones or stones, studying them as if they'd never seen such things before.

When the work was done, I sat at one of the tables and watched my father as he took time to check with each one of the passengers and speak a few words or pat a back or two. He was repaid for his attention with smiles and looks of such devotion that I was almost envious.

"He's a good 'un, ain't he, boy?" Reverend Sam appeared across the table from me and slid me a can of beer freckled with bits of crushed ice. He inclined his head toward my father and repeated his question.

I popped the top, took a sip, and studied my old man as he strolled from person to person. I shook my head.

"Hell, I don't know what he is anymore, Sam. Or who he is. Until last night I could've answered your question, but I can't anymore. I just can't"

Sam laughed.

"Hell, that's a good enough answer, boy. Better'n any I could come up with."

We sat silent, sipping our beers, until the first car loads of people began to arrive.

Sam hopped to the ground and rubbed his hands together.

"It's show time!" he yelled, and ambled off to prepare for the evening.

The message was the same as the night before and delivered to three times as many people. They sat on the ground and on the hoods of their cars or trucks. Children perched in low branches of trees. My father stood on one of the picnic tables, slowly turning as he talked, meeting the eyes of and speaking directly to everyone there. Later, when the sun had faded away, he was illuminated by a kerosene lantern scavenged from the back of someone's truck.

I watched faces and saw them accepting what he said, believing what he said. Everyone got what they wanted from his words. But there were no miracles. Just an easing of the pain. Or a gift of memories. Whatever they needed, he gave them.

Some of them cried when it was over. Some of them asked if they could travel with him when he left. No, he would say, it's good here . . . what you have here is good.

I don't think anyone left the park drastically changed from when they arrived. But I do believe every one went home and looked at and listened to the ones around them just a little bit differently. I believe most of them woke up the next morning and found the things they'd always thought of as mundane to be worthy of, if not a lot, maybe just a little bit of amazement. I don't think they'll walk through this world ignoring it anymore.

So maybe I'm wrong.

Maybe there was a miracle or two.

They'd left behind gifts of food and drink. And just like the night before, we built a fire and got the old ones fed and medicated, then tucked in their tents.

And as sick as most them were — I could see it in their eyes mostly — there were no complaints of pain from anyone. In fact, they all seemed more concerned with my well-being than with their own. And there was an air of . . . of anticipation of sorts throughout the whole camp. I don't know why, but it was almost like a feeling of Christmas Eve to a kid. A wonderful waiting.

Once again I took my place around the fire, joining my dad and Reverend Sam and Miss Emma while Carl stood watch. And though I'd only done it once before, I felt part of an age-old ritual, part of the tribe. It was as comfortable to me as breathing.

The conversation this night wasn't as dramatic as the one before. No souls were bared. There was no weeping. I didn't even try to dance. We just talked, way past the setting of the moon. And I woke the next day slumped in my chair, covered by a blanket and with a pillow tucked behind my head.

The following three days and nights were pretty much the same: travel, camp, and preach. The only difference being that everyone except me and Miss Emma and Carl got a little bit weaker, a little bit sicker. It took longer for my dad to deliver his message, with him having to stop every sentence or two to draw deep breaths. And he delivered it to crowds that grew larger each night.

But on the third night, when I finished my camp chores and took my place beside the fire, there was a definite change of attitude in my partners.

"We have to talk, Blue," my old man said as I sat. "There are some things we need for you to do. Things you might not like, things you're likely to have problems with, but we need your help, nonetheless. How about it?"

The others were looking at me as if they were about to pounce. It made me nervous.

"How about what?" I asked. "I can't give you an answer to a question I haven't heard yet."

My dad looked like he was having trouble speaking. Not like he couldn't . . . like he didn't want to.

"Aw, hell, Austin!" Reverend Sam brayed. "Just tell the boy! He's pretty much gone along with everything else up to now, ain't he? Just tell him."

The old man scuffed his feet in the dirt then took a deep breath. "You've got to give Miss Emma and Carl your car. They're goin' their own way in the mornin'. You're gonna have to take over bus-driving duty. For at least a day, maybe two."

I was shaking my head before he finished speaking.

"I've already gone over this with Miss Emma," I said, shooting her a glare. "The car's not mine and I promised to return it. Nobody's driving that thing but me." I told them how I came in possession of the Caddie and how much it meant to its owner. When I mentioned Dawson, Carl's face lit up like I'd just given him money.

"I got people there," he said. "I'll get that car back to him, Blue. I promise you. I'll get it back in good shape, too."

Miss Emma was standing beside him, patting his arm and cooing. Me and my dad and Reverend Sam were shocked into momentary silence by the first words we'd ever heard the big man speak.

I found my voice.

"I appreciate that, Carl, I really do," I told him, shaking my head, "But I can't do it. I'm sorry. Besides, this doesn't make any sense. Why are we splitting up?"

"Tell him, Austin," the Reverend said.

My dad opened his mouth to speak, and when he finished I stood up and began to back away.

"I knew it! I knew it," I said. "Y'all have all lost your minds! I'm not having any part of this anymore. As a matter of fact, I'm leaving right now. I'm going to find the nearest hospital and get help for these people. I should have done this when I first caught up with y'all. This little trip's going to end right here!"

They were all grinning at me like the crazy people they were when I felt an arm encircle my neck. During my rant Carl had flowed up behind me and now held me in an unbreakable headlock. I began to choke and he eased up a bit, still holding me tight. He dragged me back to the fire.

Reverend Sam and Miss Emma were laughing like lunatics and my old man had a faint smile upon his face. Not able to speak, I tried to plead with them with my eyes. It didn't work, though.

"Just listen to me, Blue," the old man said. "This is the only way things are going to happen. Don't you think I've thought this out? Sam here doesn't want a hospital and neither do the rest of us." Reverend Sam was nodding in agreement with my dad while still grinning at me, greatly amused.

"Everyone of the folks on the bus," my dad continued, "has told me this is how they want it to be. Hell, they came up with the idea. And, I'll admit, it took me awhile to get used to it. But it's the only way, Blue. Help us, son. Help us do this thing."

"Uh, uh," I mumbled through an attempt to shake my head. "Uh, uh."

Reverend Sam jumped up and stood before me.

"I'll take care of this," he declared.

And the Reverend began to preach.

He preached fire and brimstone, hell and damnation, slowly pacing back and forth in front of me and Carl, who stood steady, never moving. He preached every sermon he'd ever preached in what was left of that booming, Reverend Sam voice. At the end of each one he'd stop and peer into my face.

"Had enough, boy?" he'd ask. "You gonna do what your daddy wants you to do?"

And as much as I was able, I'd shake my head "no."

But the Reverend had more. And when he was done with all he had, he started over.

During this time, if I strained my eyes up and to my left, I could see my dad and Miss Emma sitting and sipping, seemingly unconcerned. Occasionally, Miss Emma came over and patted Carl's forehead with a towel and put a glass of water to his lips, ignoring me.

"You okay, baby?" she'd ask, then bat her ancient eyelids at him.

And finally, after a few minutes shy of six hours, I sagged between Carl's body and his barrel-sized bicep. They'd broken me.

"Ngh nu nah," I mumbled.

Reverend Sam stopped and cupped a hand to hear.

"What's that, boy?" he asked. "Did you say somethin'?" He motioned to Carl, who released me, and I fell to the ground.

"I'll do it," I gasped. "I don't like it, but I'll do it. I'll do it."

They helped me to a chair and gave me a drink. I drank it all and asked for another.

"Y'all are all assholes," I said.

"Ain't it the truth," said the Reverend, laughing.

My old man reached over and squeezed my shoulder.

"Thank you, son," he said. "Thank you."

The next morning I gave Carl instructions about filling the tank and cleaning the carpets. I hugged Miss Emma, then watched them ride away. She waved like hell for awhile, then turned to look at Carl. The last I saw of them she had her head upon his shoulder.

I started to pack but the old man told me to leave it all.

"We won't need it anymore," he said. "Maybe somebody else can make some use of it."

Everyone boarded the bus, talking and laughing, then sat with expectant looks at me. I pulled the door closed and turned the key and patted the gas. The big steering wheel and the sheer size of the bus took a few miles for me to get used to, but eventually I fell into the rhythm of the ride.

My father navigated, directing me through a dozen small towns. The passengers spent the day as if they were on their way to camp or some other wonderful destination. As confused as I was, I couldn't help but be cheered a bit by their attitude.

Late afternoon came and I took a right onto my old friend Highway 45. My heart was hammering in my chest as if it wanted to leap out ahead of me.

And when the sun touched the top of the trees, when the day had reached the part I liked best, we came upon the sign that read:

WELCOME
TO
DURA, GEORGIA
Pop. 2880

I grew excited at the thought of pulling the beast I was driving to a stop in front of the Tattooed Rooster Bar and Grill and being welcomed in by Elmo like some returning hero. My dad would go on display to the rest of my family while I gestured like some game-show model. With my mission accomplished, I'd sit for a while, sipping beers and graciously accepting pats on the back for a job well done.

It was not to be, though, and I knew it. We skirted the main part of town and turned right onto a seldom-used gravel road called Lula Lane that dead ended at a rusty, chain-link gate. Above the padlocked chain, hanging askew, was a peeling sign: Dura County Sanitary Landfill. Below that sign was another: CLOSED by ordinance 234-B76 June 12, 1978.

Before I could stop, my dad laid his hand on my shoulder.

"Just ease on through, son," he said.

I nosed up to the gate and patted the gas, breaking through easily enough. The gates scraped horribly against the sides of the bus as I crept into the old abandoned dump, and I winced at the sound. There was only thirty feet or so of clear road inside the entrance. I stopped and turned the bus off and could hear the passengers shuffling up front to crowd behind and peer out the windshield.

What we saw was an alien landscape of mysterious mounds covered in kudzu and obscured by weeds. Here and there, winking at us with the last of the day's light, we could see bits of colored glass from years of broken bottles. And scattered all around us, like the bones of an abandoned city, were the bulks of rusted refrigerators and stoves and other ancient appliances.

I turned in my seat to see the people behind all smiling. My dad reached for the door lever but I stopped him by placing my hand on his.

"Are you sure about this?" I asked him.

"Yeah," he said, smiling. "As sure as anything I've ever

done." And he pulled the door open and began to help the others off.

I sat alone for awhile, watching through the windshield as they all toddled around the old dump bathed in light from the bus. Exclamations of discovery and laughs of delight painted the air as they picked through the old junk, holding prizes aloft only to discard them to continue the treasure hunt.

I exited the bus and began collecting old desks and dressers and busted crates that I piled up and set fire to. The job kept me busy, not allowing me to think. And when I finished, when enough fuel was stockpiled to last the night and the fire was roaring and jumping and leaping, I noticed my dad and Reverend Sam and all the rest of the riders had gathered round to watch me.

One by one the men and women came up and hugged me or kissed my cheek and smiled secret smiles at me.

Reverend Sam took my hands.

"You awright, boy," he said in a whisper. "You a good 'un." The little man was crying a bit as he moved away.

My dad stood before me all aglow with firelight and with that new look upon his face, that look of contentment. It's funny how, now, that's the look I always remember. He wore it well.

"Tell 'em I went easy," he said to me. "Tell 'em I finally found out what this world is all about. And tell 'em . . . tell 'em I hope they find out, too." He hugged me then and I hugged him back.

That one hug made up for all the others we'd never gotten around to.

I didn't speak; I couldn't. And when my father pulled away and looked into my eyes, we both knew there was nothing else to say.

All the others made themselves comfortable in a ring around the fire. I sat down a few yards away and leaned back against an old, worn out tractor tire, waiting.

One of the old ladies began to speak in a trembling, wispy voice that became stronger as she talked. And when she finished, another took a turn.

That night they opened up that old box of toys and tossed the magic dust around, let it rain down upon them. There was still plenty there. Always had been.

And they talked . . . my God, they talked. Not about glory or forgiveness. Not about pain or things they'd meant to do. They talked about first kisses and of hazy days bathed in memories. They talked about babies being born and the best chess pie they ever ate. Way into the night they talked.

And as I was nodding off, I heard my old man begin to speak of a day when he was twenty-five-years younger and I was three feet shorter and together, on a summer Sunday afternoon, we took an endless ride along a red-ribbon road.

It was the best ride.

When I woke, they were all gone.

Chapter Fourteen

—

So, I've done what I said I'd do. The bodies are buried and the words have been spoken.

And I hurt. Both physically and in some way I can't define. All I know is how painful it is to lose someone I never really even knew, someone I'd always secretly admired. Someone I took a ride with.

One hell of a ride.

And, with all the places I have to go, I'm sure I'll ride again.

But not now. Not just yet.

I think I'll walk awhile.